MOONSHINE

By Marisol Charbonneau

ARCANA ELEMENTS

Arcana Elements is an imprint of Arcana Creations.

Cover design by Pat Bellavance with art elements under license by Can Stock Photo. Editing by Pat Bellavance.

Legal Deposit, Library & Archives Canada, June 2021

ISBN 978-1-9993954-7-6

www.arcanacreations.com

Chapter One

"Jesus Christ! Not the bloody Oracle again!" Mia protested aloud as she perused her work emails on her embarrassingly antiquated smart phone. Fortunately for her, and all the deities whose names she often muttered in vain at all hours of the day, the small Indian restaurant was mostly deserted. She had agreed to meet an old friend there as the lunch rush was still a full hour away. Mia bit her lip, not knowing if the kindly, elderly restaurateur behind the counter heard her low-key blasphemy, or whether he charitably chose to ignore his sole customer's odd outburst as he went about his business.

Once the blood ebbed away from her cheeks and restored her face to its usual pallor, Mia took a moment to compose herself. At least it wasn't the space orgy people.

Goddess be praised.

Neomia Thorne, or Mia to her intimates, always thought of herself as a reasonable woman, with sensible expectations in terms of career goals and how to achieve them. She knew when she accepted the job offer at *Goddess Digest Magazine* a couple of months ago that her aspirations of becoming a hard-hitting, award-winning journalist would have to take a backseat for a little while, perhaps even a few years, until she cut her chops in publishing. At the time she figured it couldn't hurt to work as a staff writer for an internationally known, eco-feminist Pagan publication with a wide distribution network until a better opportunity presented itself. However, she never foresaw the degree to which she would need to endure the company of a certain class of gurus, cult leaders, and probable escaped mental patients, while presenting their ramblings in a serious and professional manner to an otherwise respectable and open-minded audience.

But it wasn't all that bad, Mia thought as she warmed her hands on the oversize coffee mug set before her by the forbearing restaurateur. She drained the remainder of her coffee in one swallow, resisting the urge to scry her fortunes in the scattered grounds at the bottom of her mug. At least the job paid adequately, Mia pondered. It also helped that her oddball employer insisted that her staff live rent-free in the possibly antediluvian, city-block-size mansion inherited from some equally eccentric relations decades ago. Besides, most of the so-called journalistic grunt work fell to the overeager interns, of which Mama Willow Moon Raven Rhiannon the Wise, or whatever the hell the owner and editor-in-chief of *Goddess Digest Magazine* called herself these days, possessed in abundance. Mia figured that she could tolerate a few more years of this surreal arrangement, by which time she expected to repay her student loans in full. She could also figure out a way to undo the mess she'd made of her professional life from the point she took leave of her senses and enrolled in graduate school – a decision she considered the worst she made in her forty years thus far.

Indeed, it could have been so much worse, Mia resolved as the magic bean brew began to take effect. At least Mama Willow, in her boundless wisdom, or in a fit of picayune irony, decided to assign the annual interview with the local chapter of that space orgy cult for the upcoming Beltaine edition to that new girl, Mary Jane what's-her-name. Rumours around the communal kitchen stove at Mama Willow's claim the new girl used to be nun. Mia chuckled at the thought of the restive, too-old-to-be-an-intern thirty-something failed novitiate trying to keep her cool while faced with the disarmingly friendly acolytes of the new religious movement that put the venerable city of Montreal on the map for all the wrong reasons.

Ah well... to each their own, Mia mused. She recalled when she almost drove off the bridge connecting her home city of Montreal to the suburban-heavy South Shore after glimpsing upon a billboard advertising the cult's core beliefs. Though barely seventeen years old then, Mia never forgot the image depicting a trio of grey aliens landing upon God's green Earth, bearing a message of peace and unity, as the true face of the Divine. After almost meeting her maker following that jarring experience an embarrassing number of years ago, Mia seldom gave the space orgy people much thought. That is until her employer introduced her to a few members of the group at last month's Equinox party. They all seemed like a nice bunch of people, really, and they gave good hugs. One might even deem them mostly harmless, were it not for the rumours of the High Pontiff's unnerving tendency to recruit underage girls into his fold under the pretext of liberating them from prudish societal sexual mores.

So yes, another asinine exchange with that ditzy Oracle instead. Lady Pythia was a local celebrity medium who recently grew into a veritable flash-in-the-pan Internet sensation. It constituted a small mercy in comparison, even if at the best of times interviewing her felt like atoning for crimes committed in past lives long forgotten. Or maybe I'm just too old for this dreck, Mia considered, as the prospect of spending another afternoon in the company of this woman, a child really, loomed before her. If the Oracle were some fraudster with an uncanny ability to fool the distraught and the desperate souls who came to seek her advice, then perhaps Mia might begin to understand the cause behind her success. As far as Mia could guess, Lady Pythia was, in fact, so unskilled at interpreting omens that the spirits purportedly gave up on showing her signs and instead possessed her from time to time to give messages directly to her rapt clientele.

Mia almost became a believer the last time she interviewed the Oracle, when the latter insisted that Mia's fate, and that of her fellow human beings, would become tied in the coming months with that of the eternal and ever-shining silver Moon. Then, without explanation, Lady Pythia changed the subject to that of her childhood spent in the hills just south of Montreal, playing alone with her spirit guides in the shadow of the region's famed apple orchards. This episode might have warmed Mia to the idea that psychic mediums were, at the best of times, little more than failed therapists who could cold-read their clients, were it not for the fact that her own Greek mother named her after the waxing Moon. Lady Pythia could have easily confirmed this through a quick Internet search on the meaning of baby names. Truth be told, Mia cared not a whit about how Lady Pythia acquired her improbable gift of foresight, nor her thinly veiled attempts to impress her interviewer to elicit a positive portrayal of her services in the media. As long as she reported upon the Oracle's meandering brain farts in a way that kept the readers interested, Mia would remain in Mama Willow's good graces, and in the upstairs suite of her employer's home on the Plateau-Mont-Royal.

Glancing at the time display on her archaic smart phone for what seemed like the tenth time in as many minutes, Mia wondered where the hell Alex was. It wasn't like Alex to show up late to any of her appointments, no matter how inconsequential, and she certainly would never dare to do such a thing in her own law practice. Alex only made Mia wait when she was annoyed with her for some reason, yet they hadn't seen each other in over a year. Perhaps Alex never quite forgave Mia for the abrupt and unceremonious way their short-lived romance ended all those years ago. Then again Mia thought this quite unlikely, as their bi-curious fling happened when they were both so very young and immature. Still, youthful folly notwithstanding, even they should have known better than to base their romance on their mutual love of vegetables and vegetarian restaurants. Alex's boyfriend at the time spurned those restaurants to the point of almost contracting scurvy by the end of his freshman year. Mia's own newly remarried ex-husband, on the other hand, hardly ever touched food that came out of the Earth, yet he somehow managed to cheat death from acute constipation throughout his adult life. If social media were to be believed, he was now thriving and happily employed at a successful gaming start-up. Maybe *he* was a Witch, Mia mused. A real one, unlike some of the posers who now shared her hearth and home – a situation that would remain less than ideal for the foreseeable future.

There was no way Alex was angry with her, Mia concluded. Otherwise she would not have asked her to meet in this little vegetarian restaurant all the way out in Verdun, a working-class neighbourhood near downtown Montreal. This was where they used to sneak off to meet when they were coeds. Though their studies and professional choices caused their life paths to diverge wildly, she and Alex had remained good friends throughout the last two decades. Alex had no rational cause to punish Mia for bygone offences nor to pettily flaunt her success in her face. Though only two years Mia's junior, Alex was now an accomplished lawyer, consulting for governmental agencies on at least two continents in the field of space law. All things considered, Alex represented all that Mia hoped to become once she grew up, if such a thing were ever to happen. Beautiful, perfect Alex, whose very name, Alessandra DeBeck, painted a picture with soft Italian vowels and clipped, Teutonic syllables, of the sophisticated intelligent woman Mia foolishly repudiated all those years ago when she came to terms with her irrevocable and immutable heterosexuality.

Maybe I should have been a space lawyer like Alex, Mia pondered wistfully. Then again, she never knew until Alex went to graduate school that there was such a thing as space law, and that one could make a living legislating the heavenly bodies and the expanse beyond.

Speaking of heavenly bodies…

As if on cue, Alex hurried up to the front door of the small restaurant, making a show of her haste. Mia raised an eyebrow as Alex removed her raincoat and hung it on the rack by the entrance.

"Hey," Alex said when she finally spied Mia sitting by the window. "Sorry for the wait. Parking was a real bitch."

"Too good to take public transport like the rest of us plebes?" Mia joked, though with an edge to her voice. She made a mental note to soften her tone as it wasn't Alex's fault that her current professional and living arrangements required her to give up her own moribund vehicle and use the city's unreliable buses and subway system, or rely on coworkers giving her rides on the company cars instead.

"Look, I'll level with you," Alex said, ignoring Mia's comment. "We can't stay here for long –"

"Uh, what the hell, Alex?" Mia replied. "*You* were the one who called me. You sounded kind of weird. What's going on with you?"

"Okay, *I* can't stay here for very long, and what I have to tell you I can't really talk about out in the open –"

"*You* asked me to meet you here, in Verdun of all places, when we could have met closer to your place in Westmount right up the hill, or even downtown!" Mia retorted with the edge back in her voice. "Not cool."

"I was hoping we could speak in my car," Alex replied. "Where we could be alone."

"Whatever you have to tell me," Mia said, "Sanjay over here will likely take it to his grave, and then to his next incarnation."

Alex turned her gaze towards the affable restaurateur behind the front counter. The old man said nothing, smiling instead as he placed quarters and loonies in the cash register.

"Look," Alex said. "Let me pay for your coffee. I already got lunch."

"Wha –"

"I called twenty minutes ago."

"I've been here for only ten!" Mia protested

"Sanjay!" Alex said in a clear, authoritative voice to the old man at the cash. "I'll take my order to go. The one with the two vegetarian combos A, one bill. Thanks." Looking back at Mia, she added, "I'll explain everything, I promise. But not here."

"Fine," Mia acquiesced. "I'll take extra napkins then."

Alex chuckled. "Good," she said. "I had my car washed just last week!"

"Good thing that I'm not wearing white pants!" Mia added as she grabbed her backpack and jacket off the window ledge.

Chapter Two

"So," Mia said, wiping her mouth with the last remaining napkin as she finished her meal. "What the hell, Alex?"

Alex threw Mia a quizzical, sideways glance.

"I mean, what couldn't you tell me in a deserted restaurant in front of Sanjay, who has seen our love blossom and wilt over the years?" Mia added with a hint of humour as Alex handed her the take-out bag to throw away her napkin and her empty food container.

Alex smiled a little. "I apologize for all the cloak-and-dagger, but this has to do with work."

Mia raised an eyebrow. "You're into espionage now? Damn, girl. Are you trying to make the rest of us look like underachieving losers!?"

"I wish," Alex replied with a theatrical sigh. She stared dreamily out the driver's side window, taking in the grey April midday light as well as anyone could at this time of year, when the very notion of spring seemed only a merciful suggestion of things to come.

"Well?" Mia inquired after a moment, finding Alex's contemplation too long to endure.

"How's the new gig at the Pagan rag?" Alex asked Mia nonchalantly. "Those hippies treating you okay?"

"Uh, yeah?" Mia responded with some measure of surprise. "Not my first choice as a place to make my talents known, but so far, it's working out… Sure, life at Willowdale can get flaky and chaotic on a good day, but we've managed to go a whole month without someone threatening to do a snow dance to upset some of the cry-babies at Marketing!"

Alex sniggered despite herself. "Willowdale?" she asked. "Really?"

"Yup."

"I'll bet you a vegan cheeseburger that you didn't come up with that name."

"Nope, that was Allen, the IT guy," Mia answered as she folded the lip of the paper bag and handed it back to Alex. "He's been there forever. Great guy, you'd like him. He's got a bit of an urban yogi vibe thing going, and he's about the only person in the entire city block who doesn't bitch about April snow. So for that, and for always being there when Mercury threatens to go retrograde," Mia added with an emphatic eye roll, "he's my new best friend, present company excluded, of course."

Alex's smile waned. "I'm glad to hear you're doing well at your new job," she said almost absentmindedly.

"How about you?" Mia inquired. "I haven't seen you in a while! How the hell have you been? I had to hear from the Internet that you levelled up and got hand-picked by *the* John Sotero to be his own personal attorney at LuNation Mining International!"

"Yeah," Alex replied. "Something like that."

"Are you kidding me? That's huge! Congratulations by the way. Hey, did he ever take you to space on that rocket ship if his? It's been in the news."

"The *Aries* shuttle is still a prototype, but yes, he's taken some of us for a company outing last fall," Alex answered modestly.

"Very cool," Mia swooned. "The closest thing I ever got to space travel was last week, when my roommate Erinna celebrated 4/20 by adding a special ingredient to the chocolate cupcakes when it was her turn to make dessert. Not a whole lot of work got done that evening at Willowdale, expect for the article I wrote before going to bed. I thought it would turn out goofy, but when I read it the next morning, it was out of this world!"

Alex bit her lip to suppress her grin. "Oh Mia, you were always such a lightweight!"

"Only for the wacky weed, not the grape," Mia said. "Hey, that piece I wrote that night would have made the editorial were it not for the stupid assignment I have to follow up on this afternoon. Lady Pythia, Oracle to the stars, except that this is Quebec so the stars who make it big don't actually live here, unless they speak only French. So, yeah, that's what's going on with me."

"Yeah, I read the first part of that interview in the Spring Equinox issue," Alex confessed. "You sort of came off as a bit snarky depicting that fortune-teller, but I guess presenting such a... *character* in a fair and balanced manner ought to provide evidence as to your journalistic prowess."

"A *character* is the least snarky way to describe her," Mia grumbled caustically. "Wait a minute, you read *Goddess Digest Magazine*? What, do you sneak copies and read them inside your legal journals at the office?"

"Actually, yes!" Alex answered cheerfully as she cranked the car heater up a notch against the creeping dampness. "You have no idea how repetitive the entire body of space law from the United Nations can get! There comes a point in my day when I have to floss my brain with something completely different, and your airy-fairy flower child publication does the job."

"I'd have thought that *Goddess Digest* would fit right in at your office," Mia said, "if the rest of your co-workers follow Sotero's lead, what with the whole Capitalist Philanthropist thing he's got going."

"Don't forget mad scientist!" Alex added with good humour. "John has a reputation to uphold vis-a-vis all of us mere mortals!"

"If I heard it right, he's a Mad Scientist Capitalist Philanthropist who wants to wean the planet off fossil fuels by colonizing the Earth-facing side of the Moon and covering it in solar panels so that it looks like a disco ball!" Mia chuckled. "That can't be true... Is it?"

Alex shrugged as her laughter died down. "That's oversimplifying it a tad, but yeah, essentially," she said. "Except that he means to cover most of the middle of the surface of the Moon. There is no Earth-facing side to speak of."

"What?" Mia asked. "What about the dark side of the Moon? The side we never see on Earth?"

"Technically there is no dark side of the Moon. The Moon does a complete rotation upon its axis every 27 days and some change, but to us it looks like it's always facing the same side, which is why some believe it is tidally locked. But it's not."

"Huh," Mia replied. "I didn't know that. And I live with people who literally worship the Moon as a goddess."

"Wonders never cease," Alex jested. "But no, seriously, placing solar panels all along the Moon's equator, to absorb sunlight regardless of which side is facing the Earth, and then beaming the energy back down to the surface is not a new idea. Sotero just happens to have the resources to make it happen before the heat death of the universe, or climate change, casts us all in eternal darkness."

"Aww, so you did read my articles," Mia quipped.

"Your prose is unmistakable, but seriously... John isn't planning to turn the Moon into a disco ball, unless R&D figures out a way to produce ultra-sensitive photovoltaic solar panels that can be placed closer to the poles, but even that's a stretch."

"That's awesome, I guess? Don't get me wrong, if Sotero can actually pull it off, then more power to him, but that still sounds like something a British spy movie villain would do during their day job."

"Yeah, about that," Alex said reservedly. "There's something I have to ask, if you don't mind. And if you can fit it into your schedule."

"Are you kidding me?" Mia retorted. "You know for a fact that I'm about the interview the Queen of the fruitcakes this afternoon, and that this will constitute the height of my career for the season, right? Look Alex, how long have we known each other? If you need a favour, all you have to do is – "

"I need a favour," Alex interrupted. "And I need the full extent of your investigative skills for the task at hand."

"My hippie dippy investigative skills?"

"Your unassailable discernment and thoroughness in all your under-takings," Alex answered. "Besides, as a novice journalist, this might give you an opportunity to expand your professional horizons beyond Goddess Digest Magazine and – "

"Throwing me a bone?" Mia asked. "How charitable of you."

"I am being entirely serious," Alex answered, her tone solemn and genuine. "You may have heard about the troubles that LuNation has run onto with a certain member of a certain right-wing party among our friends south of the border?"

"Well, yeah, sort of. It's been in the news, but – "

"Then you know *why* Senator Ethan Charles has been using all his political clout to undermine John Sotero from going live with his lunar and asteroid mining venture in recent weeks?"

"I've heard that he's had issues of a moral and religious nature with regards to mining the Moon for rare earth minerals and such, but no one takes Senator Charles seriously, at least not on this side of the border," Mia answered. "The guy's obviously a religious nut job!"

"Well yes, he is by Quebecois standards," Alex replied.

"Which is why our hero Sotero chose our humble province, with its collective hard-on for secularism, as his home base of operations?" Mia retorted. "If you need me to write a fluff piece about how great your boss is –"

"No, it's nothing like that," Alex replied. "I don't need you to write poems of praise about John –"

"Then what kind of services exactly does your employer expect me to perform?" Mia asked bluntly.

"We need you to investigate Senator Charles and find dirt on him."

"Are you making fun of me Alex? Because April Fool's was three weeks ago!"

"Look, when John asked me to find a private investigator, I immediately thought of you," Alex insisted. "Senator Charles has it in for him, and he wants to get at the root of the matter so that we can address it properly in order to launch LuNation with as little fuss as possible."

"And he wants me to only investigate this Senator Charles clown?"

"Yes!" Alex answered, as if at feigning exasperation.

"Say that I accept this assignment. You understand that I have to do it way below the radar, right? Because I can lose my job over this. I have an exclusionary agreement with my current employer for the next couple of years."

"John and his wife have very deep pockets," Alex replied. "They are ready to compensate you generously for your services, as long as you perform them *way* under the radar, as you've just said."

"Say that I find dirt on Senator Charles. What will Sotero do with it?"

"We want you to find out things about him, unsavoury things, until we have enough to confront him and shut him up indefinitely," Alex answered.

"And you told your boss that I'm the woman for the job?" Mia asked incredulously.

"You have the talent, and to be perfectly frank, no one would ever suspect you of having an axe to grind against one of the most powerful men currently active in American politics."

"But why would Sotero care about what one lone American nutjob thinks about him?" Mia asked. "Maybe our neighbours to the south haven't quite figured it out, but Canada is still its own separate, sovereign nation, and the province of Quebec has long yearned to be seen as such on the international scene."

"That's true," Alex replied, "however you seem to underestimate the clout that the American government possesses over the Canadian space programme to this day... I mean, you've heard about the Arrow?"

"Yes, Jesus!" Mia cried out, almost banging her hand on the dashboard. "Everyone this side of the 49th parallel has heard of the death of the Arrow, and how Avro's loss ended up being NASA's gain! So what exactly are you implying here? Does Sotero suspect that Senator Charles is having his minions sabotage LuNation by poaching their best space talent and recruiting them to American companies? That's a bit of a stretch, don't you think?"

"We're thinking it's something far less... *pragmatic* than that," Alex answered. "We know for a fact that he's being disingenuous about his publicly rendered beliefs, and that other factors are driving his posturing against us. And we also know that Senator Charles has it in for John, not just because the U.S. is lagging behind in terms of scientific literacy and competitiveness on the world stage, but also because John represents the face of progress and philanthropy. You know how it is. The American press devotes so much of their time and resources reporting on Senator Charles' ramblings that we are left with no other choice but to strike back by exposing the extent of his callousness to the media. That's where you come in."

"But Alex," Mia protested. "You know that the American media only gives him the time of day because it brings up their ratings. And I'm only a novice reporter. You know I don't have the clout to bring him down, even if I actually find dirt on him and his office!"

"You have connections with people in high places in law enforcement, if I'm not mistaken."

"If you mean the Mounties, then you have to understand that I worked for them for only a few years while studying journalism at the University of Ottawa. That was over a decade ago! I wouldn't be surprised if most of the people I used to work with have all retired by now – which means half of them are probably already long dead. They don't tell you this in the recruitment videos, but a lot of veteran cops die within a year of retiring, for some reason or another. I'd be lucky if the rookies I happened to work with at the time are still around."

"But, if you have to, you can call in a few favours," Alex said. "Unless I'm mistaken, a lot of people nearly swore to avenge your honour when you were barred from becoming a cadet on a bullshit technicality. You have that effect of those macho white-knight types – especially the women!"

"What exactly does your employer expect me and my friends on high horses to find out about Senator Charles!?"

"Bad things, illicit things," Alex replied as she grabbed her impeccably organized briefcase and began rummaging through its contents. "In fact, John would like to discuss the matter with you personally. Here –" she produced what looked like a glossy leaflet with graphics depicting Sotero's famous *Aries 1* shuttle against a lunar landscape covered in machines hard at work installing vast arrays of solar panels on the barren Moon.

Mia took the leaflet. "A launch party?" she asked skeptically. "Isn't that a bit premature?"

"No one's ever accused the boss of being anything but a hopeless optimist," Alex answered. "Here, he also asked me to give you this –" she added, handing Mia a thick brown envelope. "I appreciate that you need some time to consider this fully, but I will need an answer sooner rather than later. The number you can reach me at is in the envelope."

Mia untucked the flap of the envelope and took a look inside to find Alex's business card. Her breath caught in her throat when she glimpsed the rest of its contents. She then looked up at Alex, her eyes wide with shock.

"This is a small token from John to compensate you for your time today," Alex said, a look of victory animating her usually placid features. "This is only a fraction of what he would pay you if you accepted our offer. At least come with me to the launch party this weekend as my date, and I'll introduce-you. Worst case, you'll spend a Saturday evening rubbing shoulders with titans of industry and enjoying some premium wine and sushi."

Mia took one last look at the envelope before putting it into her backpack.

"I'll definitely be in touch," she told Alex as she opened the passenger-side door of the car and stepped off onto the curb.

"I'll pick you up at six on Friday at Willowdale," Alex said finally as she turned on the ignition and lowered the passenger-side window for Mia to hear her clearly. "I'm taking you shopping for a cocktail dress. Dinner's on me."

Mia stood dumbfounded as Alex pulled her car away and sped towards downtown Montreal, until the sedan disappeared in a maze of recently erected construction cones and detour signs. As her gaze lingered upon these orange-coloured harbingers of Montreal's legendarily awful road repair season, Mia felt an odd throb in the pit of her stomach. She felt strange overall, though she knew her tasty vegetarian lunch could not be the cause of her unrest. Heading back towards the nearest subway station, Mia chose to put all unsettling thoughts out of her mind, save for one: the interview with Lady Pythia that afternoon did not stand a snowball's chance in hell of outshining this utterly surreal exchange with her old friend.

Chapter Three

By the time Alex presumably reached the busy streets of downtown Montreal, Mia emerged from the Snowdon Metro station at the heart of the Cote-des-Neiges borough. This was on the other side of Mount Royal, the city's eponymous hill that locals call a mountain. She headed a few blocks west on Queen Mary Avenue towards Decarie Boulevard and crossed the overpass above Autoroute 15. Mia made a beeline towards the coffee shop on the other side of the yawning chasm that passed for a highway in this less than opulent neighbourhood. Stepping inside, Mia was glad to be finally safe from speeding cars accidentally splashing her with torrents of rapidly melting grey snow. Even if the franchise coffee shop lacked by far the homey, mom-and-pop charm of Sanjay's restaurant back in Verdun, this was one of Allen's favourite haunts. Located only a stone's-throw away from the access road of Autoroute 15, one of the most direct highways to the hilly and cottage-ridden woodlands of the Laurentians north of Montreal, this was the place where Allen would soon pick her up. Mia would be taken in the company van up to the Laurentian town of Saint-Sauveur to meet Lady Pythia for their scheduled interview that afternoon.

Standing in line to purchase a small cup of hot chocolate to go, mostly as a courtesy to the franchisee, Mia looked outside the grimy window to one of the establishment's few luxuries – the parking lot. This was the main reason why Mia often met Allen in this place in the middle of the day when she needed a ride. It was also because the streets in this area were broad enough to double-park one's vehicle without compromising the already precarious traffic flow in this neck of the urban jungle. Allen's undying love for the shop's doughnuts probably also had something to do with why he often found himself in this particular location, even if he was living at Willowdale on the Plateau on the other side of the city. Despite her annoyance at having to come halfway across Montreal to meet her housemate, Mia had the good sense to keep her opinions on Allen's fondness for baked goods to herself. Allen was one of the few friends Mia had at Willowdale, save perhaps for her spirited roommate

Erinna, and he unfailingly let her vent her frustrations whenever he drove her to her assignments beyond the city limits.

Knowing full well that Allen would arrive at least half an hour late as was his custom, Mia pulled out her venerable laptop from her bag to review her notes from her last interview with Lady Pythia. While the sluggish machine booted up, she checked her emails and messages on her phone, in the hope that someone, anyone really, possessed the kindness to conjure up a reason to pull her away from her interview that day. Finding none to speak of, Mia resigned herself to the task at hand and, heaved a weary sigh as she clicked on the office server icon on her desktop.

We will get through this, she almost said aloud to the protesting brain cells of her long-suffering frontal cortex. *Just like we got through grad school. If we make it through the day without flipping tables and beating money-changers at the Oracle's parlour, I promise I will marinate the lot of you in a bath of tequila and triple-sec when we get back to Willowdale.*

As Mia closed her eyes to welcome the incoming wave of serotonin, someone knocked on the glass somewhere in front of her face on the other side of the slush-encrusted window. She opened her eyes and spied a very pale young woman, sporting a glorious mane of neon pink and purple hair, waving at her from outside the coffee shop, while Allen awaited inside the VW Minibus near the exit of the parking lot.

"I'll be out in a second!" Mia told Erinna as she gathered her things in her bag and ran a quick mental check to make certain she had not forgotten anything. Once outside, she slid open the back door of the van and climbed inside, trying her best to catch the half dozen empty cans of pop as they rolled onto the asphalt. "That was quicker than usual," she said once she collected the errant cans and tossed them back inside the vehicle.

"Exactly twenty-three minutes!" Allen answered with his usual composure.

As far as Mia knew, Allen M. Ford's personality came with two specific settings: an impassive, Zen-like calm, and what Allen himself jokingly referred to as his "inner angry black man". Though Allen was by no means famous in the conventional sense, somehow everyone knew who he was within Mama Willow's vast network of Pagans, Druids, and other Earth-centred religionists. It took him no time at all to figure out that being the only person of colour living and working at Willowdale made him stand out among anyone loosely affiliated with the Pagan community well beyond the broad distribution network of Goddess Digest Magazine. Every time Mia joked with him that her own Mediterranean heritage also made her stand out among the lily-white, mostly Anglo-Celtic denizens of Pagandom, Allen would remind her that Canadian winters made her porcelain complexion as pale as that of an Irish girl for most of the year – an inadvertent form of ethnic camouflage he could never cultivate to his benefit.

"A new record!" Erinna declared in a loud, cheery voice. "We just drove west from the Main onto des Pins and Cote-des-Neiges, then Queen-Mary. It helps that it's the middle of the day, and too late in the season for snow clearing and too early for heavy construction. It would have taken just as long just to reach the highway, so we chanced it."

"Good call," Mia mumbled as she moved the empty paper bags of take-out off the back seat with one hand and tried not to spill her full cup of hot chocolate with the other as she sat down and shut the door beside her.

"We thought you would want to get this done as soon as possible," Allen replied. "And Erinna offered to tag along to give moral support."

"Boss Lady knows you're here?" Mia asked Erinna.

"Yeah, I told her you might need help rehearsing your interview questions beforehand, so she gave me her blessing to tag along," Erinna answered. "Frankly I think she's afraid you're going to call Lady Pythia a wanker and a fraud and stuff like that while you're there, so it wasn't hard to convince her that you needed adult supervision."

Mia bit her lip. "Have I ever threatened out loud to do such a thing?" she asked earnestly.

"You sometimes kvetch in your sleep," Erinna replied.

"And anyone within a three-kilometer radius of the energy circle that surrounds Willowdale can sense your contempt at anything to do with the Oracular arts," Allen added.

"I don't mind astrologers and psychic mediums who use their craft in a therapeutic context, the kind that genuinely helps people deal with their shit," Mia said a bit defensively. "But I do take exception at the ones who are loopier than my breakfast cereal, because those people can cause real harm, even without meaning to. And Pythia, well, I'm not a doctor, but even I can tell that she needs to have the people in white lab coats and clip boards take her away for a little while, for her own good. But what do I know?"

"More than most," Allen answered as he slowly pulled the van out of the parking lot and made a hard right onto the southbound lane of Decarie boulevard. "Just sit tight. Barring traffic, an accident, or Erinna having to go pee again, we should be in the Laurentians in less than an hour."

Mia put the cup of hot chocolate to her lips and took a sip.

Goddess give me strength.

"This too shall pass," Allen said offhandedly as he zigzagged through the bumpy side streets flanking the highway to reverse course to head north onto Autoroute 15.

"You would not believe the morning I've had," Mia said unhappily, holding her mostly full cup in such a way as to avoid ending up wearing her beverage, and instantly regretting her habit of forgoing plastic lids for environmental reasons.

"Oh?" Erinna inquired, spinning around to face Mia.

Mia bit her lip, remembering the fat envelope in her backpack and her own admonition for discretion were she to accept the mysterious assignment. "I had lunch with my friend Alex," she said, trying to sound vague and wistful. "My beautiful, successful, accomplished friend Alex, who's younger than me and has her own house in Westmount, last time I checked, and probably spends her weekends eating vegan caviar and sipping champagne in an Armani bathrobe."

"Don't waste your energy comparing where you are in life with other people," Allen opined. "That way lies madness, baby girl."

"You are so wise," Mia replied facetiously as she took another sip of her hot chocolate.

"You can't always measure success by your purchasing power," Allen continued. "Besides, isn't Alex your friend who legislates space balls?"

Mia spat out her drink.

"Space balls!" Erinna howled, bursting into laughter.

"Alex's specialty is the *Agreement Governing the Activities of States on the Moon and Other Celestial Bodies*," Mia answered once she caught her breath. "That's literally the name of the U.N. Treaty dealing with forthcoming exploration and mining rights to places like the Moon and planets and asteroids. And they're not all spherical, by the way!"

"That's... esoteric to say the least," Allen commented. "How the hell did she manage to get a job specializing in *that*?"

"It's the way of the future," Erinna answered before Mia could reply.

"If that were true," Allen continued, "teachers and guidance counsellors would be telling children to go into space exploration instead of becoming doctors and lawyers and shit."

"Alex is a lawyer," Mia said. "A good one, actually. Hence her legislating space balls, as you mentioned."

"Right," Allen replied. "But still. You can't feel bad because you don't have a fancy mansion in Westmount in the hills with a pool where the neighbours' dumb-ass drunk kids sneak into in the middle of the night and end up drowning. Or with those driveways up at a forty-five-degree angle where you risk your car rolling all the way down to the river if you forget to put your parking brake up. Really, you're better off at Willowdale, baby girl. Most of these rich folks work so many hours in a week that they don't even get to enjoy their expensive fancy crap anyway!"

"The rest of the time they're chasing their cars down the hills," Erinna added.

"Come on guys," Mia said, suppressing a smile. "That has literally never happened. Probably."

"That's because the potholes in Westmount are large enough to swallow cars or at least slow them down before they hit the river."

"Wouldn't all those cars end up in Verdun, on the other side of Autoroute 20, before they could even get near the river?" Mia asked skeptically.

"What do you think they use to fence out all the sharks from those new beaches they're constantly building down there?" Allen replied. "I'm telling you, if you scuba dive far enough from the shore, you'll see a wall of last year's BMWs keeping those man-eating motherfuckers at bay!"

"I know you're only trying to make me laugh," Mia said.

"And it's working!" Erinna added. "Feel better?"

"Yeah," Mia answered, as the Minibus crawled onto the ramp towards the gloomy trench constituting the northbound Autoroute 15. "And here we go."

"It will be over soon," Allen said.

"Isn't that what they tell people who are about to get enemas?" Mia inquired sardonically. "I mean, seriously though," she continued when neither Allen nor Erinna gave a response. "Is this what I went to graduate school for? To become a platform for nutjobs to spew their nonsense to the masses? I mean, have you two ever asked yourselves, what *are* we doing?"

"We're doing our job?" Erinna answered hesitantly.

"Yeah," Allen agreed. "We're giving the readers what they want. Lady Pythia is popular these days, and articles about her sell magazines, so that's why the nice kooky lady who runs the magazine from her Covenstead sent us to visit the other nice kooky lady who lives in that witch's cottage up there in the mountains."

A cottage she paid for by defrauding gullible idiots, Mia thought, though she had the wisdom not to complain aloud lest Allen lecture her further about gratitude and the impermanence of material things.

"Every good journalist has to start somewhere," Erinna said unhelpfully.

"At rock bottom," Mia muttered under her breath.

"Where you build the strongest foundations," Allen retorted.

"Okay, fine," Mia conceded. "I'll interview the freaking Oracle. Just try not to run over any Munchkins on the orange cone road or crash your van on her sister. Last time I was there the neighbour looked like she wanted to steal her shoes!"

"Uh oh," Erinna said as the Minibus made a full stop on the highway.

"What is it? Mia asked.

"Gridlock," Allen answered. "The sign over there says there's an accident somewhere on the access to the 40 east."

"Can't we exit at Jean-Talon and take the 40 closer to Rockland?" Mia asked.

"No can do," Allen replied. "We already passed that exit. Looks like we're stuck here for a while."

"Oh no," Mia retorted, barely concealing her glee.

"Should we call the Oracle to tell her?" Erinna asked.

"You mean, there's a chance she didn't see this coming?" Mia mused aloud, knowing full well that both Allen and Erinna would ignore her comment.

"You should text Mama Willow to let her know," Allen told Erinna. "She should be the one to tell Pythia that we might be late."

Please, Goddess, Mia thought, *let there be a dozen cars piled upside down on the access ramp so that we're stuck here long enough for the interview to get cancelled... but let no one be seriously hurt, of course.*

"Okay, hold on," Erinna said as she fished her phone out of her coat pocket and did as Allen instructed. After a moment, she spoke up again. "Willow said to stay the course but also to give her status updates every fifteen minutes." Turning to face Mia, she said, "she also wants to know if your phone or laptop have teleconferencing capabilities, in case Pythia is open to doing this by video chat or conference call."

"That's a hard no for either," Mia answered truthfully. "Both my devices are absolute relics. And tell her that I'm a little miffed that she did not give me the option of doing this interview by phone to begin with. The universe could have been spared a lot of bad vibes if she'd opened with that. Hell, tell her that the car accident causing this traffic jam is a probable consequence of my anxiety-ridden morning! No, don't tell her the last part. She usually takes me at my word when I use hyperbole for effect."

"Words have power, baby girl," Allen chided Mia in a friendly manner. "So do thoughts."

"If only," Mia replied, her thoughts trailing off into the aether as an idea formed into her head.

This is a sign from the Universe.

Mia took a deep breath. She closed her eyes as her free hand slipped inside her backpack until her fingers brushed against the fat envelope Alex gave her only a few hours prior.

What are you doing here? You are here to expose the truth about the source of all evil in this world, and to do your part in making things right when you find out what it is.

That is why you were chosen, and that is why you chose this profession to accomplish this Great Work.

"Mia? Are you okay?" Erinna asked casually after a moment.

Mia opened her eyes and pulled out her laptop from her backpack. She drained the rest of her hot chocolate in one swallow, placed the empty cup between her feet, then fished out the power cord for her ancient computer with her newly free hand.

"I'm fine," she answered as she handed the power cord to Erinna to plug into the battery pack tucked away in the glove compartment. "I'm just going to do some quick research in the meantime, if you guys don't mind. I might rework that editorial I wrote last Saturday, in case the Oracle interview falls through."

"Okay sure," Allen replied, "but Lady Pythia's website is an Escheresque nightmare!"

"I know," Mia answered casually.

But LuNationMiningInternational.com is not.

Chapter Four

At long last, the improvised parking lot in the grey, unsightly cement ditch that passed for the northbound Autoroute 15 stirred to life. Presumably, the emergency response teams finished sorting out the car pileup ahead. Mia had no idea how long she and her teammates had been stuck in traffic – not that she cared much, given how much hope this interlude provided her on this otherwise dreary day. Still, Mia felt a bit guilty for ignoring her friends who sacrificed their afternoon to tag along and boost her spirits, while she spent her borrowed time researching a potentially lucrative extracurricular opportunity. Mia supposed that perhaps her companions interpreted her silence as an integral part of her process. Like many of the various writers, journalists and other creative types among whom they dwelt and worked, Mia's best ideas usually came to her without warning. Maybe Allen and Erinna thought that the Muses had planted a seed of an idea inside Mia's mind, and therefore let her work in peace lest the fragile spark of insight go out like a flame stolen in a fennel stalk from the very heights of Olympus itself. Mia said nothing, thinking it would be best for her friends to persist in the belief that she was currently drinking from the wellspring of inspiration bubbling forth from the very depths of Creation, or something terribly poetic to that effect.

This vehicular imbroglio must have been the work of Providence, Mia thought as Allen restarted the engine of the Minibus once the cars ahead started to move consistently enough. It was the middle of the workday on a Wednesday, after all. Why were there so many cars on the road on the northbound Autoroute 15 in the first place? Mia often thought of midday traffic jams in Montreal as a religious experience of sorts. It was a phenomenon no one could quite explain, yet undeniable in its manifestation. If this interview were to be postponed, hopefully indefinitely, Mia pledged to offer a libation to the deities governing Montreal traffic, whoever They may be, as soon as she returned home.

On second thought, perhaps she ought to thank the traffic gods for their favour later in the evening, after she properly thanked her comrades for being such good sports about the whole misadventure. So it was settled; after dedicating the first batch of margaritas to Allen and Erinna, Mia would pour an offering of the delicious concoction before the tree in the communal garden, where other denizens of Willowdale habitually thanked the Powers that Be for their charmed existence. But it would have to be a saltless margarita, Mia considered, because salt is bad for plants. Then again, maybe alcohol is bad for plants as well; it's not exactly great for humans, save for killing germs during flu season, which in Montreal lasts from September until May. After some reflection, Mia concluded that perhaps margaritas do not, in fact, constitute an appropriate offering to the traffic gods, for reasons including but not limited to their chemical composition.

It will have to be coffee and granola bars, or whatever else remains of tomorrow's breakfast, Mia resolved. If the squirrels eat it, then I will know that the gods have accepted my offering. Then again, exposing squirrels to vast amounts of sugar and even a small amount of caffeine might be an even worse idea, given the innate restless nature of the tiny, twitchy rodents.

"Oh, bloody hell," Mia muttered under her breath.

Offerings are hard.

"Calm your tits!" Erinna said while thumbing the screen of her smartphone. "No need for cussing, I just got a text from Willow. She said that the interview is a no-go for today. We'll reschedule later this Spring, maybe early June, as Lady Pythia has back-to-back engagements throughout May."

"This is your lucky day, baby girl," Allen told Mia as he drove the vehicle onto the exit ramp towards Autoroute 40 east.

"So what now?" Mia asked, bracing herself against her seat while the Minibus merged with the heavy traffic with the grace and manoeuvrability of a brick.

"Right now, we grab some groceries at *Marché Central* before heading back home," Allen answered. "Mary Jane is still on assignment at the commune – you know which one, and won't be able to pick up the tofu in time for vegan General Tao tonight, so we have to make a pit stop."

"Here we come to save the day!" Erinna sang cheerfully off-key in response.

"You're too young to know the reference," Allen scolded her good-naturedly.

"I have Internet-foo!" Erinna protested. "And I'm a career receptionist-slash-administrative-assistant. I can find out just about anything!"

"You okay back there?" Allen asked Mia, ignoring Erinna's reply.

"Yeah, I'm good," Mia said. "I will have to also make a pit stop at the SAQ, if you guys don't mind."

"The Society of the Alcohols of Quebec?" Erinna asked, badly translating the French acronym for the government-run liquor dispensary on purpose.

"Yeah'" Mia answered. "I need to pick up a couple of bottles of tequila and triple-sec, and then I need to go to a hardware store to grab a few packs of wildflower seeds for the garden. You know, for the bees?"

"Look at you, making offerings to the Earth-Mother like a boss," Allen said with a smile in his voice.

"Our little girl is growing up," Erinna added with mock wistfulness.

"Very funny," Mia replied.

"I suppose the booze is to be shared with the rest of the class?" Allen inquired.

"Of course!" Mia answered. "Besides, I figured that Mary Jane might also need some spirits to bleach her brain after her interview with the House of Interstellar Intercourse, poor thing."

"You know, I think Mary Jane is way more resilient than you give her credit for," Allen said as he exited the highway. He drove the Minibus onto a side street to reach the vast parking lot of the *Marché Central*, an extensive strip-mall complex at the very centre of the Island on Montreal with an even more extensive parking lot that always seemed full at all hours of the day.

"You're probably right, as usual," Mia replied. "So, where to first?"

"The booze, then food," Allen answered. "We'll need to skip the hardware store if we stand a chance at beating traffic on the way home. It's that time of the year, they should have packs of wildflower seeds by the checkout at the grocery store."

Of course, O Wise one, Mia thought.

Acquiring the various provisions across the vast expanses of the *Marché Central* while avoiding the newly formed potholes and slush lakes proved a rather simple and effortless task compared to that which lay ahead. For all Mia knew, Mama Willow was planning at that very moment to give her an even more inane assignment than the last one, which was only postponed for a blessed month or so. Even if her assignment with Alex' employer proved mercifully short and fell far beneath her true capabilities, Mia would still need to cover her tracks credibly should her employer catch her in the act of moonlighting as an investigative journalist for a multinational, extraplanetary mining consortium.

As the Minibus meandered artlessly through the maze of one-way streets on the way back to Willowdale, the Muses graced Mia's pineal gland with a brilliant idea: that of casually pitching to Mama Willow a story culminating in a hard-hitting exposé on the harmful effects of right-wing Evangelical Dominionism in politics and society. As a faith-based publication, Mia could argue that such a story would fall well within the scope of *Goddess Digest Magazine*, especially if presented in a well substantiated manner. Moreover, this story could provide an opportunity for the magazine to give readers a break from the usual feel-good fluff, and maybe even challenge the dangerous ethos of unconditional acceptance so prevalent in the wider Pagan community.

Confident that her plan would enable her to hit two birds with one stone, Mia scrambled frantically to gather her discarded disposable cup of hot chocolate, as well as other detritus left behind by slovenly co-workers in days and weeks past. Working up the nerve to pitch the story to her notoriously stubborn editor-in-chief, Mia almost leaped out of the Minibus as soon as the vehicle pulled into the narrow alleyway towards the small parking lot behind Mama Willow's posh manor. Mia disregarded Allen's quip about having a fire lit up under her ass all of a sudden, and almost body-checked Erinna as the latter slid the rear passenger side door open and began to hand the groceries to Luna Rowan Moonbeam, *Goddess Digest Magazine's* senior copywriter tasked with cooking tonight's meal. Mia would have to give her friends a second glass of delicious margarita to offset the accidental slight lest her karma catch up to her, she thought as she made a mad dash towards her quarters on the third floor of the manor. Once there, Mia carefully plugged in her depleted smartphone as well as her energy-hungry laptop into their respective chargers, then grabbed her trusty notepad in which she scribbled her ideas in bullet form before committing them to the printed page.

Mia looked at the digits displayed on the alarm clock on her bedside table.

Five-thirty. Dinner will be served in half an hour. If I'm pitching this story today, it will have to be after dinner. Or during dinner if Willow deigns to ask me what I plan to do now that the interview with Lady Pythia is on the back burner. Stranger things have happened.

Mia barely noticed when Erinna entered their shared quarters to call her for dinner.

Showtime. Here we go.

Marisol Charbonneau

Chapter Five

Mia entered the vast dining parlour, eager for once to stand in line before the serving table with the rest of the live-in staff of *Goddess Digest Magazine*. As per Willowdale custom, each awaited their turn to fill their plates and take their places at the communal table. Mia did not mind waiting for her meal, for she knew that Luna's cooking talents were disappointing at worst, and insufficient at best in terms of transforming soy blocks into anything resembling a flavourful dish. In fact, Mia learned to divest herself of her vice of gluttony as soon as she moved under Willow's roof. It wasn't only abandoning the consumption of meat that caused her to inadvertently shed ten of her extra thirty pounds – one of the few outcomes she did not regret since casting her lot with *Goddess Digest Magazine*. It was predominantly the realization that very few practicing vegetarians and vegans, and even fewer among her coworkers and housemates, shared Sanjay's culinary virtuosity for meatless fare.

Low gastronomic expectations notwithstanding, Mia eventually took a plate off the stack by the edge of the serving table and grabbed a modest portion of vegan General Tao. She then took a seat near the middle of the long table, where Erinna and Allen usually sat with Othmane, the unfailingly polite and endlessly amused Moroccan intern comprising the other half of the I.T. department. A devout Muslim, Othmane often seemed out of place at Willowdale; Mia suspected that the lad only took the job in the hopes of regaling his relatives back home with fantastic tales of his tenure at a real, honest-to-god, Covenstead. Mia enjoyed Othmane's enthusiasm and curiosity for all things witchy and countercultural, however this evening she would refrain from spirited discussion and wait instead for her chance to pitch her idea to Willow should the opportunity present itself during a lull.

This will be tricky, Mia thought. Now that the die was cast and her decision made, she could not allow anything to break her resolve, not even Willow's glaring resistance to story pitches deviating from her editorial comfort zone. Perhaps the spiel could wait until after supper, once hunger pangs were abated even by a sub-par approximation of an Americanized classic Chinese dish.

Or better yet, maybe I ought to ply Willow with a generous helping of magical gratitude margarita, to put the odds in my favour.

Mia halted, her fork almost stabbing her lower lip as she pondered her latest abstraction. Truth be told, she had not once seen Willow inebriated. This was perhaps a function of Willow's notorious control issues in all aspects of her life, which unfortunately for her staff did not safeguard anyone from her extraordinary propensity for random flights of fancy in her editorial duties. Willow's egregiously *inspired* notion of assigning Mia to interview the Oracle came to mind as an example of the latter.

"Pondering the mysteries of the soy?" said a childlike voice.

Mia looked up, stirred from her irreverent contemplation, and saw Erinna, Allen, and Othmane clustered in front of her on the other side of the table. The trio were deep in conversation, discussing the improbable topic of the use of letters in Western script by Arabic-speaking Moroccans while texting.

"You've been staring at your fork for, like, ten minutes now," said the voice. "Did you guys inhale lots of exhaust fumes in the van?"

Mia spun around and saw Hekate, Willow's young daughter, sitting in a spot left vacant by members of the advertising crew who likely finished their meals and left the dining parlour.

"Katie," Mia answered. "I didn't hear you come in."

"Dad just picked me up from school," Katie said. "He was working late at the university, and I had rehearsals, so it worked out."

Mia craned her neck and spied Philip Raven, Willow's committed life-partner and father to Hekate "Katie" Willow Song Raven, taking a seat by the head of the table where Willow sat. Mia gave him a little wave, which Phil returned almost immediately before attacking his full plate. It never ceased to amuse Mia how Phil ended up with someone like Willow, and unwittingly became the catalyst behind Mia's employment at *Goddess Digest Magazine*. Mia had known Phil for years, since they were both undergraduates at Concordia University. Concordia was an institution of higher learning that only recently outgrew its reputation as the red-bricked, unholy love child borne of the merger between a blue-collar night school at the heart of Montreal's downtown core and a defunct Jesuit college in the city's west end.

Back in the day, Phil Raven (and yes, that was his real name) was a student in physics and Mia, an arts major of course. He was also the roommate of Mia's ex-boyfriend at the time. When Phil found out about Mia's fling with Alex, he agreed never to tell his flatmate about the indiscretion, mostly out of pure human kindness and decency, and also out of concern that the young man might fall ill with scurvy before the end of the semester. Mia and Phil had been close friends ever since and became in-laws shortly after graduation when Phil married Mia's older sister, Hestia. Phil and Hestia's union, however, was short-lived as the couple divorced a few years later after trying and failing to get pregnant. Strangely enough, Phil met Willow through Hestia, who by the time of their separation had become highly involved in Neo-Pagan circles before converting to orthodox Judaism and changing her name to Hester.

Mia always thought that Phil and Willow made for a terribly mismatched pair. Phil was an easygoing, unflappable tenured professor of physics at McGill University, one of Canada's most prestigious Ivy League schools and a veritable ornament presiding majestically atop Montreal's financial district as well as Mount Royal's southeastern slope with its stately buildings and manicured lawns. Willow, a product of McGill's plebeian anglophone rival, Concordia University, was a kind and affable High Priestess in the eclectic Celtic Wiccan tradition inherited from her ascended Masters in the magical land of Tír na nÓg, or Atlantis, or something to that effect – Mia never paid much heed to Willow's so-called esoteric pedigree. Willow also possessed a terribly flighty and overbearing disposition, which made her short-sightedness as editor-in-chief of a somewhat respectable ecofeminist pagan publication even more difficult to endure for someone like Mia, whose tolerance for mercurial types waned exponentially with each passing day.

"Are you going to eat that?" Katie asked Mia.

Mia looked down at her half-eaten plate, then at the growing child looking back at her.

"You can have it," she answered. "I'm done."

"Thanks," Katie said, piling Mia's food into her own empty plate.

Mia chuckled. "You look like you need to consume animal protein," she whispered, so that the girl's mother could not hear.

"Oh, Dad took me out for burgers at lunchtime," Katie replied. "He cut his office hours short so we met at a diner on McGill College Avenue one block from both our schools. He said I needed the energy if I stood a chance at nailing that solo at rehearsal. But don't tell Mom!"

"You know me better than that!" Mia protested, giving the child a look of mock disappointment.

"Right," Katie said with her mouth full of General Tao not-chicken.

"Speaking of which, I have to have a talk with your Mom later."

"If it's about the Oracle, better wait until morning," Katie replied. "Mom has it in her head that you sent bad vibes out in the Universe because you've been in a crap mood since your first interview with Lady Pythia, and that your negativity had something to do with that nasty car pileup on the 15."

"You know about that?" Mia asked.

"It made the news! The accident, not the interview. One of the drivers removed their winter tires too early and skidded on black ice. I mean, how else does a car end up upside down on a highway this late in the season?"

"So it really was a freak accident?" Mia mumbled.

"Yeah!" Katie answered. "Good thing no one got hurt! Those guys should buy a lotto ticket!"

"And your Mom thinks that my reluctance towards my assignment had something to do with this?"

Katie nodded.

"Huh, I wonder what gave her that idea?" Mia said, turning her head towards Erinna to throw her an accusatory glower.

"It wasn't me!" Erinna protested before Mia finished her slight head pivot. "I didn't text her that after you told me not to!"

Allen shook his head. "Don't even think it!" he said.

Mia sighed. The magical gratitude margaritas would have to wait until she found the true culprit or until someone confessed to snitching. Nevertheless, she would have to conjure up a reason to claim the communal blender from the kitchen before those twerps from advertising returned and grabbed it for themselves, so she devised a cunning plan.

"If you will all excuse me," Mia said, rising to her feet. "I do believe it's my turn to load the dishwasher –"

Before Mia finished her sentence, Erinna, Allen, Othmane and Katie handed her their empty plates in a neat pile, with the utensils stacked on top. Other denizens of Willowdale followed suit, until the dish pile became comically high.

"You guys know I don't *actually* have the strength of ten men, right?" Mia asked the stragglers sarcastically.

"Come on now," Willow interjected. "We can all bring our plates to the kitchen. Then I'm certain that our dear Mia will share her magic brew with those who help her clear the table!"

Mia blinked. *What the hell*?

"Yeah," Mia said after a moment. "But it'll be a one-drink maximum, otherwise I'll deplete our salt supply and have to use the consecrated salt in the temple pantry."

Erinna chuckled and helped Mia divide the tower of plates into smaller piles as Allen, Phil, and a few others carried the stacks into the kitchen. Katie rose to help as well, however Willow stopped the barely teenaged child before she could rightfully claim her reward of a salty margarita on a school night. To Mia's surprise, Willow joined the cleanup effort, stacking a ridiculously high pile of dishes into her dainty hands and carrying them beatifically into the kitchen with near preternatural force. Mia always thought it unsettling how her boss, a comely, waifish blonde who likely weighed exactly the same as a duck, could carry out such feats of strengths while putting Mia's own impressive brawn to shame. Mia put these thoughts out of her mind as Willow began to rinse the dishes and hand them to Mia to load into the empty dishwasher while the others busied themselves bussing the rest of the serving bowls and cutlery onto the kitchen counters. Once the evening chores were done and the leftovers put away in the manor's three refrigerators, Mia opened the doors to the walk-in pantry and searched for the bottles of spirits she had purchased that afternoon. She could not remember if she brought them upstairs, or whether Erinna put them away with the rest of the groceries when Mia ran out of the Minibus earlier like a bat out of hell.

"Top shelf, to your left," Willow called out from the kitchen, as if hearing Mia's thoughts. There were times when Mia could swear that Willow knew how to read minds, especially her own. It was mildly unnerving when Mia was sober. The rest of the time, it was downright spooky.

Mia grabbed her bottles and returned to the kitchen with a plastic container of salt, then placed her quarry next to the unplugged blender. "How many do you want?" she asked Willow.

"None for me, thanks," Willow answered.

Mia looked around in the kitchen, then out into the dining parlour, which was now deserted. "Where did the others go?"

"They're all hanging out in the basement with I.T. I think they're having a game night. I told them to go ahead and get started while we finish up here."

"Oh?" Mia said, a tad annoyed that Willow would presume to answer on her behalf when they were off the clock.

"I got the feeling that you wanted to talk," Willow said.

Mia stared at Willow for a moment.

There it is again. Wait, don't think! She might hear you.

"Sure?" Mia replied tentatively.

"Look, I know you're not too happy with the Oracle assignment-"

"I did not send funky vibes into the Universe to cause that car crash," Mia interrupted her hastily. "Besides, no one was injured, or so I've been told."

"Goddess be praised!" Willow replied patiently. "But that's not why I wanted to talk to you. Mia, look. I know you haven't been happy with the assignments I've given you of late, but you must understand, we have a way of doing things here, and your colleagues have seniority. That's why I give you the beginner-level assignments. It's not a comment on your abilities, far from it. It's just how we operate. You'll see, if you keep up the good work, like I know you can, soon you'll be one of our top contributors –"

"What if I told you I have a great idea for a story?" Mia asked excitedly. "I mean, not a fluffy-bunny feel-good double-rainbow hippy-dippy trippy filler piece, but an actual investigation, that deals with issues and engages with our readers at a whole new level?"

Willow raised an eyebrow.

"Hear me out," Mia continued. "What if I were to infiltrate those conservative Evangelical Dominionist groups that try to pull at the strings of the most right-wing factions of our federal and provincial parties – we could start just with Quebec. No, wait, scratch that. Our right-wing nut jobs are not religious here. Never mind. Just the federal parties. I could infiltrate these groups, you know? And see what makes them tick, and expose their motivations for attacking the hard-earned rights of women and minorities, the LGBTQ, and whatnot, and do an exposé to … *expose* them, and mobilize our readers to go out and vote and resist the encroachments of their rights and freedoms guaranteed by the Constitution of our great nation –"

"Let me stop you right there," Willow said flatly.

"Well, what do you think?" Mia asked expectantly.

"No."

"What, no?" Mia replied incredulously. "Hard no?"

"Hard no."

"But… why? Willow, it's a great idea, and right up our alley as a Pagan publication! It's the sort of investigative journalism teen magazines have been doing since our neighbours to the South lost their collective minds a few years ago!"

"Your idea reeks of intolerance against our fellow human beings who happen to think differently from us," Willow answered firmly. "And it breeds divisiveness, which is something I cannot condone. The mission statement of *Goddess Digest Magazine* is to bring people together and foster community through fellowship and shared values, which is extremely difficult to do among Pagans. So far we have been able to do just that by writing our, how did you call it, feel-good double-rainbow, hippy-dippy material and we will continue to do so, as long as I'm the one running this publication."

Mia's mouth fell agape.

"Frankly, I'm disappointed in you, Mia," Willow continued. "You are getting way ahead of yourself. You need to learn to crawl before you learn to run, and the story idea you just gave me proves that you are not ready. I'm going to reassign you at reception for a couple of weeks to help out Erinna with her filing backlog until I trust that you have come to your senses. Now, go ahead and make those margaritas for the others downstairs and enjoy your game night, but remember that our administrative offices open at eight-thirty. I expect to see you at the front desk at that time, not after ten like you usually show up for work or whenever you feel like it. So don't stay up too late. Good night."

Willow turned her heels and exited the kitchen, leaving Mia utterly speechless. Once she knew she was well and truly alone, Mia grabbed her unopened bottles and climbed the stairs to her flat. She shut the door behind her, unplugged her laptop and placed it carefully into her backpack, then dialed a number from memory on her still-charging smartphone, taking deep breaths as the person on the other end failed to answer after the first three rings.

"Yeah, hi, it's me," Mia said finally when a familiar voice answered. "Look, I'm sorry, I know it's late, and this is unexpected, but can I stay with you and Ira for a while? It's really not working out where I am, and I need to go NOW. Yeah, can you come pick me up? A half-hour? No, you can take your time, I need to pack my things anyway. Okay, an hour. That's perfect. I'll meet you outside, there should be plenty of parking. It'll be after nine, so the meters will be free. Thank you so much, I'll see you soon. Love you."

Mia hung up and took another long, deep breath. She counted to ten, then turned on her ceiling lamp and headed to her closet, where she grabbed her suitcases neatly tucked into one another. She began removing her belongings from her shelves, reminding herself to grab her alarm clock on her bedside table once she was done packing her few worldly possessions.

By then her phone should be fully charged, and Hestia "Hester" Thorne Greenbaum, and possibly her husband Ira, will be parked across the street to pick her up and take her to their home in the tranquil, tree-lined, and heavily Hebraic borough of Outremont, on the northeastern slope of Mount Royal.

Marisol Charbonneau

Chapter Six

The hallways on the upper floors of Willowdale were mercifully deserted when Mia finally emerged from her flat, suitcases in hand and her backpack fastened to her shoulders. She tiptoed across the front parlour, quickly realizing that anyone still awake was now gaming and chatting loudly in the I.T. department lounge downstairs. It was therefore rather unlikely that anyone would hear her as she left the manor this late into the evening. Mia placed her suitcases by the door in the entry, then halted before taking her backpack off her shoulders, remembering the fat envelope that Alex gave her that morning as an advance for her mysterious assignment.

Dear gods, that was only this morning. This day cannot get any more surreal. No, wait, that was not a dare. NOT A DARE!

Mia took a deep, calming breath. Almost forty minutes elapsed since she called her sister; she might not have much time left to do a quick run-through of the common areas of the manor to retrieve whatever possessions she had left. Mia looked at her suitcases, marvelling at the ease with which she packed up everything she owned in such small, confined spaces. Mia was never much of a materialist, not since she moved away from Montreal over a decade ago to pursue her graduate studies. At the time, it felt almost liberating to cull almost all her belongings until she could fit her worldly possessions in their entirety into the trunk of her now moribund car.

The car...

The clunker was still parked in the back of the parking lot behind Willowdale, presumably sheltering mice and raccoons, and whatever urban fauna made their homes within the nooks and crannies between buildings in this part of town. Mia left it there two months ago when she moved into Willowdale, hoping that she could save enough money to get it fixed by summer. Fetching the car would have to wait until the next time Mia spoke to Erinna or another one of Willow's administrative minions when she'd finally gather enough nerve to formally resign from her post as junior writer for *Goddess Digest Magazine*. Hopefully the job with Alex's employer would pan out, and Mia would not even need her severance pay or even a letter of recommendation from Willow for her future employment prospects. If it didn't, then maybe the car could fetch a couple of hundred dollars from the junkyard – if it could start and make it out if the driveway without leaving too many small furry creatures homeless in the meantime.

All that nonsense could wait, Mia thought. Hester might be here any minute now; it would be inconsiderate to make her wait after dragging her all the way to the Plateau at this late hour. Mia slid the closet doors open, grabbed the winter jacket she left there just in case Mother Nature surprised this city with yet another late-spring snowstorm, then draped it over one of her suitcases and exited the antechamber. By now the temperature outside dropped to just above the freezing point, which at this time of the year usually felt like a welcome warm front. By late April most Montrealers became idiotically happy whenever the weather forecast called for rain instead of snow, for it meant the true end of winter when it was safe to come out of hibernation and change seasonal wardrobes and whatnot.

Mia sat on the steps of the front porch, draping her shoulders and backpack with her winter jacket. Realizing that she did not remember the make and model of her sister's car, she fished her phone out of her backpack with a practiced hand and checked her messages.

"We're parked in front of the *dépanneur*," said a text from ten minutes ago.

Mia bit her lip and scanned the street towards the little corner store embedded within a gas station franchise across the darkened one-way street but could not see any silhouettes within the parked cars.

"Turn on your headlights and flicker twice," Mia texted back. "I will come to you."

Seconds later, the headlights of a large sedan flickered twice, then a young man exited from the driver's side and waved in Mia's general direction. It must be Moshe, Mia thought, trying to remember the last time she saw Ira's youngest son. How many of Ira's children did my sister bring to assist in my rescue, Mia wondered as she grabbed her suitcases and walked across the street to the end of the block towards the car.

Ah well, the more the merrier?

Mia bit her lip again. Who was she to judge how her kind, loving elder sibling acquired her family? When Hester met Ira Greenbaum, he was a widower and a father to eight beautiful children; his first wife passed away from breast cancer when Moshe was only eighteen months old. By then, Hester was newly divorced and in the process of converting to Judaism after deciding that her long, arduous spiritual quest had led her to Montreal's venerable orthodox community. Their marriage shocked many of Ira's neighbours and relatives, though, as his new bride was only a couple of years older than his eldest daughter, Shoshanna, who at twenty-six years of age was already married with four children of her own. Nevertheless, the couple enjoyed a happy marriage, and Hester became quite close with Ira's youngest children, raising them as her own after coming to terms with her infertility, the cause of which many competent physicians could not explain.

So if this is Moshe, he must be what, sixteen or seventeen years old? He must be at least that age, otherwise he could not legally drive. Dear gods I hope Hester or Ira are in the car with him.

As Mia approached the car, a lovely, matronly woman in her early forties exited the passenger's side door and met Mia in an embrace, while her young companion took Mia's luggage and placed it in the trunk.

"Sorry I had to get you here this late, Tia," Mia said, momentarily forgetting her sister's name-change. "Hi Moshe."

"Hi aunt Mia," the lad replied.

"Mia, you poor thing," Hester said. "What happened? What did that vile *heym vrekker* do to you?"

"Uh, I'd rather not get into it right here in front of her house," Mia replied.

"Of course," Hester said. "Come, we will take you home. Take the seat behind me, there will be more leg room. Our Moshe is growing up so fast, soon he'll be taller than his father!"

"I already am!" Moshe protested as he opened the rear and front passenger doors for Mia and Hester at the same time.

"You're still a growing boy," Hester replied. "Now remember, release the parking brake this time when we pull out. We are on a flat road!"

"All right!" the young man winged moodily.

"And watch out for black ice," Hester continued. "There was a terrible accident on the 15 today, a car got flipped upside down! Thank God no one was seriously hurt."

Mia suppressed a smile as Moshe started the engine and drove the car haltingly towards Avenue du Parc, where he made a right turn and headed north. Mia remained quiet for the rest of the drive towards Outremont, taking impish delight at the spectacle of her older sister, who for most of her youth had been such a free spirit, kvetching at her stepson as if he were still a toddler.

"We will put you up in Rebecca's room for now," Hester told Mia while Moshe turned right onto Avenue Van Horne then right again onto de l'Esplanade, looping back south then westward onto Rue Bernard. Like the Plateau-Mont-Royal where Willow made her Covenstead, the comely borough of Outremont looked like a suburban bedroom community within the city of Montreal, with large single-family dwellings neighbouring a few small businesses along its sparse commercial axes. However, by virtue of being far less trendy and gentrified than the Plateau-Mont-Royal, Outremont attracted fewer hipsters and French expatriates than the former.

"When she returns from school in the summer, well," Hester continued, "I guess we can work that out when that happens."

Mia waited before answering, trying to simultaneously find her bearings in this part of the city she seldom visited – and remember Rebecca among Ira's large brood.

"Becca's the lucky one who gets paid to go play in the sand," Moshe said, kindly getting Mia caught up on the adventures of the Greenbaum clan.

"So she's still interested in archaeology?" Mia asked, recalling the bright, curious girl who was only a few years older than Moshe.

"The government of Israel gave her a scholarship," Hester answered proudly. "She's thinking of staying there for her graduate studies at the University of Jerusalem!"

"Yeah, I think they're *this close* to finding the body," Moshe added sardonically.

"Good for Becca," Mia said, resisting the impulse to laugh at Moshe's cheeky and blasphemous retort. "And don't worry, I won't be staying with you guys that long. Maybe a couple of weeks at most until I figure out a few things."

"You are welcome to stay with us for as long as you need," Hester said in an almost chiding manner as Moshe made a sharp left onto Avenue Querbes, where the family lived. "Come now, you can tell us all about it inside."

"There isn't that much to tell," Mia said as she exited the sedan once Moshe parked the car in the narrow driveway. "The gig at the Pagan rag didn't work out, but I might have another job lined up. Depends on what happens in the next few days."

"Please stick around, aunt Mia," Moshe said, opening the trunk and grabbing the suitcases. "You're fun."

"Your auntie is not here for your entertainment!" Hester scolded the boy good-naturedly. "Now bring her things inside and go to bed! This is a school night!"

Mia picked up her winter coat from the back seat then shut the door. "Thanks for the lift, kid," she told Moshe.

"No problem, aunt Mia," the boy replied before disappearing inside the shotgun house with the suitcases.

Hester bade Mia to follow her inside, closing the front door behind them as they escaped the evening chill of late spring. While Mia tried to remember how long it had been since she set foot in her sister's home, Hester turned on the lights in the front parlour, where Ira joined them to greet the new arrival.

It's been way too long, Mia thought, noticing how much her brother-in-law had aged in the last few years, long after her return from her misadventure at graduate school a decade ago. Mia bit her lip when Ira motioned to greet her, feeling a pang of regret for not visiting more often. Though the god of his ancestors proved kind by bestowing many blessings upon him – including abundant progeny and two loyal, loving wives, Ira Greenbaum did not share Mia and Hester's gift of a preternaturally youthful appearance. He did, however, possess the kind of beatific serenity endemic to a certain class of men when they neared their golden years after a life well lived.

Or it might be the study of the Kabbalah. Yeah, that's it. It's that occult magical stuff that makes him look so wizardly in his old age. It has to be. No wonder Hester felt attracted to him when she was very young; he comes from a culture when men are encouraged to literally wrestle with their god to gain a better understanding of the mysteries of the Universe...

For some reason, Ira grinned at Mia and gave her a wink, then excused himself under the pretext of retiring to bed early, even if it was by now barely past ten. Once Ira was well out of earshot, Hester led Mia into the kitchen.

"Tell me what this is really about, Mia," Hester said as she put the kettle on, gesturing for Mia to take a seat. "What did that bleach blonde bimbo poseur do to you that had you packing your suitcases and leaving like a thief in the night on a Wednesday?"

Bleach blonde bimbo poseur? There are far more colourful ways to describe the magical unicorn that is Mama Willow Moon Raven Rhiannon the Wise...

"Still sore about her and Phil, huh?" Mia asked, obviously deflecting her sister's inquiry while pacing around the kitchen table in wide arcs.

"I forgave her for that a long time ago," Hester replied. "I have no cause to complain about my lot – I have a good life with a wonderful husband and family. And I am happy for Phil that Willow gave him the child that I could not. But my grievances against her are not the point. I'm more concerned about you for moving in with a woman whose many moral failings even motherhood cannot atone for. What in the world were you thinking? If you needed a job so badly, I'm sure my Ira could have helped you out! He has a lot of influence over the congregation; people still call him Rabbi even after he retired! And God knows there is always someone somewhere who could use your talents. Even if it might not have been what you wanted at first, there certainly are better ways to make a living than to write about the professionally mentally imbalanced!"

"So... you read about that?" Mia asked with some measure of embarrassment.

"I keep a scrapbook of your articles, to tell my grandchildren about their aunt who writes stories about all sorts of people that make the world such an interesting place," Hester replied enthusiastically. "You have such a talent, Mia. You can do a lot better than working for that *woman*! I mean, have you even read some of the things she wrote before you joined her staff? She makes spirituality sound like it's all rainbows, glitter, and fluffy bunnies dancing under the full Moon, but it's not. Spirituality is about confronting the darkness within, so that you can better see the light! It's not all about tarot, crystals, shamans, and drums! Not that there's anything wrong with these things. Just because I left these things behind doesn't mean –"

"Look, I know what you're trying to say," Mia interrupted. "But Willow doesn't have any power over me. I came into this arrangement willingly, but there are some things I just couldn't put up with anymore, so I made the choice to leave. On my own, like a big girl. Honestly, I think I outgrew the place within the first two weeks of moving in. Willowdale looks good on paper, but the place is a mess! You'd think that the manor was built on the ruins of an ancient temple of Eris or something like that. I mean, they have a common room for almost everything – the kitchen, the garage, the bathrooms, but no one's in charge of making sure that any of it works. Take the kitchen – did you know that there are maybe two forks for the entirety of the household during daylight hours? I'm talking about for at least twenty people who live there full-time, and many more who come by during the day! It's true. Every time I set foot in the kitchen, there was nary a fork in sight except at dinnertime! It got so bad that some of us theorized the Willow hid the forks on purpose during the day just to make sure we didn't waste our time eating recreationally. Also, the job was totally beneath me, so yeah, my leaving was a long time coming."

"How did Willow take the news?"

"I haven't told her yet –"

"Mia!"

"No, I'm going to tell her tomorrow... I will... but first I have to talk to Alex to let her know that I am now available full-time for a job she offered me very recently. You remember Alex, right?"

"*Oy vey!*" Hester interjected. "Don't tell me you're back together with her!"

"No, no... nothing like that. We sometimes meet for lunch and chat –"

"At that Indian vegetarian restaurant?" Hester asked with a barely suppressed grin.

"Yes, *that* restaurant. But today she told me that her employer might have a job for me. I can't get into the details, it's all very hush-hush. But it involves some real, legit, investigative journalistic work to bring down the bad people and expose them, like I always wanted to do. The same kind of work that would make my entire student career worth it in the end, because I need to believe that it was all for something. Something more than fluff pieces in a Pagan magazine!"

Mia finally took a seat at the kitchen table. Hester handed her a cup of hot tea, then joined her on the chair beside her.

"Look, I know this has not been easy for you," she said. "But I need you to know that your nieces and nephews, especially Moshe, really look up to you. I tell them that you are the kind of person that the world needs, one who is guided by her morals, and who seeks to make the world a better place through her work and deeds. We have an expression for that in our faith. *Tikkun Olam* – it means to repair the world."

Mia perked up a little but said nothing.

"You have a spark in you, Mia," Hester continued. "No matter what you do, you always do what is right in the end. Maybe you need to do something right now that you didn't expect. Whatever it is you need to do, just know that we are here for you, and that our home is your home."

Mia looked down at her mug of tea.

"Thanks," she mumbled. "This means a lot."

"Don't even mention it!" Hester said reassuringly.

"But let me ask you one thing... *Tikkun Olam*, that's from the Kabbalah, right? I thought women weren't supposed to study the Kabbalah, only married men past forty."

Hester did not reply, though her smile widened.

"So, I'm kind of getting the feeling that you and Ira share more than faith and family, am I right?"

"Yes, I study Kabbalah," Hester admitted at last. "I have for years. That is how Ira and I met, actually. Neither he nor I have ever told another soul, though I have the sneaking suspicion that Moshe knows."

Mia grinned at her sister. "Oh, you rebel!" she joked, before proceeding to sipping her tea.

"Yes, well, that must remain our little secret," Hester said at last. "Can you imagine what the neighbours would say if they found out? They barely survived the news of my engagement to Ira. This might just do them in!"

Mia spat out her tea and laughed for what seemed like the first time in far too long. Maybe everything would turn out all right, she thought, making a mental note to alert Alex of her change of address first thing in the morning.

There was a lot she needed to get done before her meeting with John Sotero at the party this Saturday, and it was already past mid-week.

Marisol Charbonneau

Chapter Seven

The next morning, Mia awoke in her niece's bedroom, momentarily unsure of where she was until the previous day's surreal chain of events inundated her consciousness like the springtime high water that flooded the suburbs around Montreal this time each year. Mia took some time to fully come to terms with the fact that not only did this glorious, sunny April morning find her unemployed, she was also homeless, for she did not consider staying in her sister's house an acceptable prospect in the long term. But it could be worse, she thought. At least she had caring relatives, a warm bed to sleep in, and a roof over her head for the time being. Maybe Hester was right, in that leaving Willowdale could prove the first step for Mia to make something of herself professionally. Or better yet, maybe God, the gods, or the Powers that be, had grown as weary as she did of watching her subsist on scraps and finally presented her with an opportunity to realize her life's purpose.

Satisfied that the Universe was not, in fact, playing a cruel joke on her, Mia slowly got out of bed and rummaged through her suitcase for her hoodie or some sweatpants to throw on before heading to the bathroom. It would be improper to leave Becca's room while wearing only her T-shirt and panties, as she now shared a hearth with her devout Jewish kin, including at least one teenage boy, three of his older siblings, and their father, His High Holiness the Rabbi emeritus. As she fished for her hastily gathered clothing, Mia heard a knock on the door. She looked up and saw Hester come in, unprompted, with a stack of fresh towels and a bathrobe.

"Good morning," Mia said, somewhat relieved that her sister had little concern for her present state of undress.

"Good morning," Hester replied calmly. "Did you sleep well? Did Ira and I keep you up last night?"

"Uh, no?" Mia answered, grinning slyly. "I mean, I slept like a baby. Thanks for asking."

"Good, good," Hester said. "Here, I thought you might need these towels."

"What time is it anyway?" Mia asked, her eyes still blinking into the shafts of spring sunlight.

"It's twenty to ten," Hester said. "Oh, don't worry, I figured you needed to rest after the day you had yesterday. I made some breakfast. Come downstairs when you're ready. Ruthie and the boys left for the day, so you have the upstairs bathroom all to yourself."

"Thanks," Mia replied gratefully. "Give me about ten minutes, I'll be right there."

Once she had showered, Mia tiptoed across the hallway back into Becca's room and dressed into a clean pair of dark wash jeans, a light floral blouse and her trusty chocolate-brown suede blazer – her gift to herself for surviving the ordeal of graduate school. She would need to look professional today when she headed downtown to her bank to deposit the cash in the fat envelope now residing in her backpack. The last thing she wanted was to raise the bank employees' suspicions by looking like a derelict. Mia reached her hand into her backpack to feel the envelope, but her fingers kept catching on the contours of her old laptop. She lifted the flap of the bag and peeked inside, rummaging through its contents to glimpse upon the windfall that would constitute her safety net for the immediate future. Mia heaved a sigh of relief when she saw her quarry pinned at the bottom of the bag, wedged between her laptop and her notebook. She then saw her smartphone, its charger cord coiled in a ball. She really ought to text Alex right away to let her know about her change in employment status, she thought as she picked up the phone.

Ten text messages awaited her: two from Allen, three from Erinna, four from Willow, and one from Phil. While Allen and Erinna's texts predictably expressed alarm and concern at her sudden departure, Willow's came off as apoplectic and passive-aggressive in equal measure. Phil's message, on the other hand, simply requested that Mia call him at his office once she was awake, and maybe meet him for lunch today so that they can discuss her resignation from *Goddess Digest Magazine*, absent the publication's miffed editor-in-chief. Mia chuckled, picturing her ex-brother-in-law towing her car and whatever else she'd left behind and awkwardly dropping it in front of Hester's home, while the Greenbaum clan looked on at the procession of hippies taking him back to the Plateau. It would be best for all parties, Mia resolved, to meet Phil today and figure out the logistics of concluding her exodus from Willowdale in the quickest and most painless way possible.

We'll do lunch, she replied to Phil's message. *Meet you at twelve-thirty in front of your office?*

Come by at one, Phil texted back almost immediately. *I have office hours until 12:45 and I'll need at least 15 minutes to floss my brain until I'm ready for polite company.*

Mia chuckled. *1 PM it is*, she wrote.

The commute to downtown Montreal was blessedly uneventful. Mia took the opportunity to walk all the way down Avenue du Parc on the eastern half of the street to soak in the sunshine and breathe in the springtime air. At almost all the cafés on either side of the avenue, staff were placing tables and chairs onto makeshift terraces, a confident display of defiance against winter's last throes. Mia made it all the way to the corner of Avenue Mont-Royal, where she crossed to the west side of the avenue to walk alongside the foot of the mountain, before she stepped in a torrent of ice-cold meltwater flowing from the heights and soaked her toes through a hole in her battered winter boots. Instead of uttering a rather vile string of profanities in the French-Canadian vernacular involving liturgical items such as communion wafers and the chalice that holds the communion wine, as well as the small box holding said items, Mia took a deep breath and silently thanked her footwear for their service. She then hurried across the meadow at the foot of Mount Royal towards the maze of two-story buildings constituting the McGill University residential student ghetto, and raced across the stately campus to reach the network of interconnected shopping centres flanking McGill College Avenue to buy a new pair of shoes.

This must be a sign, Mia thought as she stepped inside Place Montreal-Trust and took the downward escalator twice to the lowest level to reach the basement, where a large budget department store would most likely carry at least one pair of newly arrived and affordably priced shoes for her choosing. Mia made a beeline towards the far wall of the store, found the aisle with her shoe size, and selected a presentable pair of walking loafers. As she sat down to try on her footwear, she noticed a constellation of slush had formed on the back of her legs on her dark wash jeans. She simply wiped the streaks away with her bare hands, knowing full well that anyone who dared to venture outdoors during spring in Montreal met the same fate. Mia then threw away her old winter boots after making her purchase, for they were in too poor a condition to donate to the needy. In a few weeks, when winter boots will be on clearance in every store, she would buy a new pair for a steal. But today, it was springtime, the time for new and exciting things. Out with the old!

Once Mia finished depositing the contents of her fat envelope at her bank, she headed back to Place Montreal-Trust and deliberately ordered an overpriced coffee at the bookstore at the corner of the building. She still had some time to kill before her lunch with Phil, so she texted back Erinna and Allen, but not Willow. Screw that obnoxious poseur, she thought of the latter. There was no point in wasting time on those who take delight in keeping others professionally underfed.

Besides, you have your whole career ahead of you. You are a real journalist. You will investigate bad people and expose them in the Court of public opinion. Speaking of which...

Alex. She had yet to text Alex.

With bated breath, Mia texted Alex the words that would change the course of her life: *I'm in. Let Sotero know I look forward to meeting him this Saturday.*

Mia barely had the time to exhale when Alex texted back: *Fantastic! Are you sure this won't cause issues with your employer?*

Mia smiled as she replied, *I quit the Pagan rag. Moved in with my sister for now, until I get my own place.*

That's great news, Alex texted back. *I'm happy for you. Look, I can't talk right now, in meetings all day. Text me your current address and I'll pick you up tomorrow at four.*

Mia bit her lip, picturing her pious relatives watching her as she absconded with her former lesbian lover into the glimmering city lights of downtown Montreal at sundown on the Sabbath.

We can meet tomorrow at four in the lounge of the Queen Elizabeth hotel, Mia replied. *It's central and close to all the nice stores.*

Ok agreed. Meet you there at four tomorrow. Allow time for parking. You know the drill. TTYL.

Drinking deeply of her egregiously precious coffee, Mia looked at the timepiece on her archaic phone. She got up quickly and gathered her backpack and blazer, then hurried down the spiral stairwell of the bookstore and out the door, knowing full well that Phil would be expecting her at the McGill Campus in less than twenty minutes.

As it turned out, the Rutherford Physics Building was located almost all the way up Robert-Bourassa Boulevard, barely more than a block from where the Percival Molson Stadium began, the latter jutting down from the slope of Mount Royal and flanked by Avenue du Parc to the east and Avenue des Pins to the south.

"Go Alouettes", Mia mused as she nearly ran up the steady slope of University Street clad in her unbroken new shoes, missing her half decomposed and discarded winter boots. As she jogged uncomfortably northward, she passed by Katie's posh arts-oriented high school to the east of the McGill campus. A pang of regret hit her square in the chest as she thought of Katie, and for a moment she could almost have sworn that she saw the girl's face in one of the windows on the third floor of the building.

Is it regret or the first signs of a heart attack? Slow down, you're woefully out of shape and you're not getting any younger!

Mia took deep breaths as she curtailed her pace, spying Phil waiting for her outside the imposing grey building housing the physics department, right next to the McGill Space Institute.

"Hey there, stranger," he joked as he walked down the steps and greeted Mia with a hug. He looked unnervingly calm, as he always did regardless of circumstances.

"Hey Phil," Mia replied.

"I know this little place in the neighbourhood," Phil said as he bade Mia to follow him eastward into the McGill residential ghetto, back into the maze of narrow streets and low-rises that Mia crossed a few hours prior. "They have a really good vegetarian menu, and I know how much you like that stuff, so I took the liberty of making reservations."

"Thanks," Mia said. "Sorry for the *theatrical* exit last night, but I needed some air."

"Willow finally got you to snap?" Phil retorted in a way that was not quite a question. "Allen and I have been running bets on how long it would take until you ran away –"

"With the circus," Mia interrupted with a chuckle. "I thought you guys *were* the circus! What have I got left to run to, a regular job with normal hours and a steady paycheque?"

"Take it from me," Phil said, weaving against throngs of students crossing into campus. "Normalcy is overrated. So where are you staying at, now that you ran away from the circus?"

"At my sister's," Mia replied.

As expected, Phil took a moment to process this. "How is Tia?" he said after walking the length of an entire city block without saying a word. "Still playing house with the silver fox?"

"It's Hester now," Mia said. "And she's happily married to the Rabbi. Has been for fifteen years now. I know, it seems like just yesterday she began delving into the roots of Western esotericism, but I just saw their youngest. He's driving! Ye gods, that made me feel my age!"

"*Oy vey,*" Phil replied facetiously. "Okay, I know I shouldn't make fun. My Katie is only a few years away from getting her driver's license."

"Maybe we should plan the betrothal," Mia joked. "To secure peace between the matriarch of the Greenbaum tribe and the Queen Bee of *Goddess Digest Magazine*?"

Phil chuckled softly. "I hope your nephew likes the artistic type," he said.

"From what I saw last night, I got a feeling they would get along just fine," Mia said half in jest. "So, just how pissed is Willow at my leaving? Should I call my brother-in-law and tell him to keep the windows closed until the flying monkey brigade has gone away?"

"It wasn't quite like that," Phil answered.

"But not good?"

"Well, it was kind of funny actually," Phil explained. "Yesterday when you were stuck in traffic and Willow called Lady Pythia to let her know about the gridlock, Pythia told her that you would soon be setting forth on a quest to safeguard the Moon for the benefit of all humanity, so there was that."

"She said what now?" Mia uttered incredulously.

"That left Willow a bit out of sorts until dinnertime, when she told me about the call. I think she got spooked and decided to reassign you regardless of what you'd done, or didn't do, just so you'd be less inclined to leave on an epic journey to save the world."

"Yesterday, Willow demoted me to office gopher-slash-filing-clerk," Mia griped. "Not that there's anything wrong with that job, but that was not what I went to grad school for."

"Oh, I know. I've always known you could do better than *Goddess Digest Magazine*, but I thought working there could help you cut your teeth until you found something better. Otherwise I would never have suggested that Willow hire you. But let me tell you, I regretted it immediately after the first time you had to interview Pythia. Here is the restaurant. After you."

"That's when you and Allen started to place bets on how long I'd last?" Mia asked as she and Phil crossed the threshold of an unremarkable building, into a shoebox-sized establishment that probably barely met fire safety standards. "So, who won?"

"Neither of us, to tell the truth. You lasted far longer than I expected, but not as long as Allen thought you would." Turning to the very young hostess behind a tiny counter at the front of the restaurant, Phil added, "Reservations under Dr. Raven, Menus in English, thanks."

The barely legal hostess bade Mia and Phil to follow her to the back of the small room, to a table wedged into a corner under the stairs between the kitchen and the washroom, and handed them two menus that looked almost as old as the little building itself. Sanjay's restaurant this was not, Mia thought, but she chose not to emote her displeasure at Phil's choice of venue. Today she would close a shameful chapter in her life, and start her career anew on the right foot with a real assignment that would prove to the world that she could cut her journalistic chops on something more substantial than fluff pieces about false prophets and lunatics.

Mia perused the menu, chose an entrée that constituted a firm departure from her preferred fare, and glimpsed at her companion, who likely made his choice long before setting foot in the restaurant.

"Hey Phil, can I ask you a question, completely unrelated to the fuckery at *Goddess Digest Magazine*?" Mia asked casually.

Phil looked up at Mia. "Sure," he replied. "But I figured you agreed to meet me today because you wanted to sort out your post-fuckery exit strategy."

"We will talk about that for sure," Mia said. "Maybe later once we've had food. But first I need to ask you a question that's well within your area of expertise. It's for a new job I'm hoping to land in the next few days. Journalism, you know."

Phil raised an eyebrow but said nothing.

"You specialize in astrophysics, right?" Mia inquired. "I mean, space stuff, actual rocket science?"

"Those are not the same thing," Phil answered. "Astrophysics is to the study of the interactions of matter and energy as pertains to stars and celestial bodies. No one is a rocket scientist, that's not really a thing, unless you're referring to an aerospace engineer. There's an element of physics to it, of course, but it's not the same as astrophysics or cosmology. So yes, I specialize in astrophysics, and no, that doesn't make me a rocket scientist."

"Okay, good to know," Mia replied. "So here's my question: what exactly, in your expert opinion, would motivate a person, say, a person in a position of power and influence, to oppose the efforts of another person or corporation to mine the Moon for minerals and the like?"

Phil pondered Mia's words for a moment. The wheels inside his head seemed to turn even as the waiter showed up to take their order, then left, then returned with two glasses of water.

"The Moon, eh?" Phil said at last.

Mia nodded.

"That's an interesting question," Phil replied. "First of all, you have to ask yourself, why mine the Moon in the first place?"

"I meant to ask that first," Mia retorted. "Why mine the Moon at all?"

"Well, the Moon has some things in abundance that we either do not have, or are running out of, here on Earth. For example, the Moon is rife with water. Water is essential for sustaining life, which is why anyone who stakes their claims to mining sites on the Moon will likely make use of vast lunar deposits of water to sustain their settlements off-world, provided that they figure out sustainable means of food production up there as well."

"Makes sense," Mia said, "but we still have plenty of water here on Earth."

"True," Phil replied. "Water can be treated and purified ad infinitum, so long as we have the resources and technology to do so, but it's highly impractical to export it to space in the quantities needed for off-world settlement, mining and exploitation. That brings me to my next point: what the Moon also has, and we are definitely running out of, are rare earth minerals. We use those in the manufacturing of modern electronics, like computers and cell phones, and as the name suggests, these are extremely scarce here on Earth. Right now, the world's supply of rare earth minerals is mostly found in China, and even there they are expected to run out within the next decade, maybe twenty years if we're being optimistic. So you can begin to see why someone of great power and influence might take exception at another interested party staking claims on a prime site of lunar exploitation if they have their sights set on getting to the Moon's riches first."

Mia nodded.

"Then there's the third thing that the Moon has that the Earth does not, at least in significant quantities," Phil continued. "That is Helium-3."

Mia almost snorted her drink of water.

"Like what the space Nazis used as an energy source in that silly indie movie from a few years ago?" she chuckled.

"That's correct, well no, there are no space Nazis on the dark side of the Moon. There is no actual dark side of the Moon, so to speak. But the scientific community agrees that there could be vast deposits of Helium-3 on the Moon, and that this resource could be exploited as a fuel for nuclear fusion, for spaceships and power plants, on Earth and on the Moon..."

"And other celestial bodies..." Mia finished Phil's sentence.

"So you are familiar with the United Nations' Moon Treaty," Phil added.

"Yes," Mia answered. "I read it once or twice, after Alex mentioned it to me for the first time, years ago. The whole thing is so repetitive that it reads like a ancient Greek poem!"

"You're not wrong about that," Phil said calmly. "So you must also know that the Moon Treaty bans any organization or person, and that includes private companies, from claiming ownership of the Moon and other celestial bodies, unless the claim is made by an international or governmental body."

"Yeah, and I sense there's a 'but' in there somewhere."

"But, as you might also know, the Moon Treaty is considered to be a failed treaty," Phil continued, "as a significant number of countries, including our neighbours to the south, have not ratified it. This means that as far as many nations are concerned, the Moon is fair game to whoever gets there first and sets up a mining operation."

"So it's a lawless frontier?" Mia asked, intrigued.

"Well, yes and no," Phil replied. "If someone were to stake a claim on a mining site on the Moon, or other celestial bodies, they would have to operate under something akin to maritime law. It's kind of like deep-sea mining and oil drilling operations today, where the installations have to operate under the laws of whichever country whose flag they fly under. Does that answer your question?"

"Yeah, it does, kind of," Mia said. "So the Moon has lots of abundant and important resources, and a sort-of clean energy source. It's also the new Wild West, only high above. But here's another question: if someone *were* to follow the rules stipulated by the United Nations in the Moon Treaty back at the dawn of the Space Race, and by that I mean joining forces with lots of international and inter-governmental bodies before staking a claim on a mining site on the Moon, would that invalidate someone else's claim on the Moon's riches if that other someone were to go at it alone? Especially if the latter insisted on continuing to use obsolete fossil fuel technology and the like here on Earth?"

"I suppose so," Phil answered.

"And so the second party would have everything to gain by placing a target on the first party's back and to drag their name through the mud?"

"That would be my guess."

"Huh. Interesting."

Phil furrowed his brow. "I don't know what you're hoping to get yourself into," he said, "but my advice would be, for whatever it is you're investigating, to follow the money. Who has it, who wants it, and who stands to lose it the most. You see, it's almost always about money, and money is power. It's not rocket science."

Mia smiled. "You had to go there," she sighed, just as the waiter returned with their plates.

"I had to," Phil retorted. "Now, let's enjoy our meal. Then we'll talk about your resignation on a full stomach. Just promise me you won't get in over you head and get kidnapped by bloodthirsty space pirates for your new job. I'd hate for that to happen."

"Yeah, that would suck," Mia agreed.

"But I know that you know a good lawyer," Phil added with a wink.

Mia raised an eyebrow. "*Bon appétit!*" she replied, taking in the fragrant aroma of her turkey burger and sweet potato fries – with a side of vegetables.

Marisol Charbonneau

Chapter Eight

Friday morning began with an eight A.M. wake-up knock on the door from Hester. For a night owl like Mia, this usually felt like the very crack of dawn. However Mia insisted upon it, for she needed to get up early and spend many hours that day researching the sorts of things she ought to know to sound competent and intelligent upon meeting the great John Sotero, capitalist philanthropist, and soon-to-be mogul of extra-planetary resource extraction. As per Phil's suggestion, Mia would spend part of the day in his office on campus getting caught up on recent developments regarding space exploration, as well as lunar and asteroid prospecting. With regards to the fallout from her exit from Willowdale, Phil assured Mia that Willow would issue her record of employment for official tax purposes and mail it to Hester's address by the end of next week.

As for the remainder of her possessions not yet collected, Erinna would canvass the manor to gather whatever was left, then return the items to Mia in a neat package that she would place in her car. Phil also assured Mia that no small creatures would be harmed while removing the vehicle from its current premises since, unbeknownst to Mia, Erinna had the car towed and stored in an indoor storage space somewhere out west in the city shortly after Mia moved into Willowdale. As it turned out, when Mia came into her employ, Willow took one look at her new hire's clunker and decided that it would be best for the Earth-Mother to put Mia's car in storage. By Willow's logic, Mia could make use of Willowdale's fleet of fuel-efficient vehicles instead of polluting the biosphere, or better yet carpool with her colleagues by making use of her electric Minibus.

When Mia found out that Willow put her car in storage without her knowledge or consent, she actually bit her tongue so as not to unleash a litany of profanities at the Witch-Queen's very patient Consort. Instead, Mia thanked Phil for finally letting her know about the extent of Willow's undiagnosed control issues and resolved to sell the rusting corpse of her vehicle for scraps as soon as she recovered it. She would then use the cash as part of a down payment to purchase a new, fully electric vehicle, provided that she could secure more permanent employment at LuNation Mining International. If Saturday's meeting went well, which it ought to, given the thickness of the envelope Alex gave her on Wednesday, then Mia would never again have to worry about money woes. Of course, all this would depend upon how much information about space mining she could absorb in a single afternoon, which also meant that she ought not to dawdle if she were to stand a chance at successfully bringing to completion the task at hand.

Now that she devised the semblance of a plan, Mia performed her morning ablutions shortly after Hester and Ira's children – young adults, really – left about their business for the day, then gathered her laptop and smartphone in her backpack and headed to the McGill University campus for the second time in as many days. Yesterday's sunny skies were now covered with low, heavy grey clouds that would bring much needed rain upon the city, which at this point in the season would prove a cause for celebration for most Montrealers, who by now had lost all patience with this past winter's ceaseless malingering. Phil was kind enough to leave Mia the spare set of keys belonging to his officemate, who was away on a joint project with the Institute for Astronomy at the University of Hawaii for another seven months to study near-Earth asteroids and mini-moons and the threat these objects pose to our continued existence. When Mia heard about the whereabouts of Phil's colleague, she immediately resisted the urge to wallow in remorse for her choice of field of studies, as once upon a time she would have liked very much to hold a profession where she could protect her fellow human beings from harm – hence her failed, long-ago attempt at becoming a Mountie. Fortunately for Mia, sometime between dinner on Wednesday evening and sunrise the following morning, she decided that self-pity was a poisoned well from which she'd pledged to never drink again. From this moment on, Mia would refrain from following this particular downward spiral that never once led her anywhere useful or good.

Instead, Mia resolved to enjoy the neat, comfortable vacant desk and chair in Phil's small office, while the latter was away giving lectures until about three o'clock, after which he would head out as it was his turn to get groceries for Friday dinner. That was fine, Mia told him, as she planned to also leave the campus around three and slowly make her way to the Queen Elizabeth hotel lounge a few blocks south of the University. On the way there Mia would step into the Eaton Centre, a multi-tiered shopping mall named after an iconic, yet bygone Canadian department store, and take the time to look at the spring fashions on display in the windows of every shop on every floor. Afterwards, she would take the tunnel to Place Ville Marie, a cross between an office building and a modest shopping centre with a ludicrously swanky food court, and then sidestep the access tunnel to the underground Central Station station for above-ground trains, and walk right into the opulent lobby of the elegant Queen Elizabeth hotel. The network of downtown tunnels turned out to be especially useful that afternoon, for the skies opened up with torrential rain shortly after three-fifteen, mere seconds after Mia accessed the mercantile anthills that constituted Montreal's financial district and underground city via the McGill Metro station across the street from the Eaton Centre. As anticipated, the rain, though abundant, made all the Montrealers idiotically happy, for it was not snow.

Mia opted not to indulge in afternoon tea at the posh restaurant of the Queen Elizabeth – or *Le Reine Elizabeth* as per the sign outside. There would be time for such extravagances once she secured lucrative employment with LuNation, she thought. For now, she would remain content sipping her ginger ale while perusing the copious notes she took that day, as was her habit whenever she did background research while following leads on a new story. She did exactly that until Alex appeared in the hotel lobby a few minutes early, her hair soaking wet, but her spirits undismayed.

"I suppose you found parking outside," Mia joked when she greeted Alex. "How far did you walk in the rain?"

"Oh, just across the one street," Alex answered, taking a seat at Mia's side at the bar. "I'm parked on Cathcart, right on the other side of Place Ville Marie. I only crossed the road and went the rest of the way indoors!"

"Okay, that's impressive," Mia retorted.

"Tell me about it!" Alex said. "It's been pouring literal buckets for half an hour now! Your pals at the Pagan magazine didn't do a rain dance, did they? Because it looks like someone's been praying for rain!"

"Knowing that lot, probably not," Mia answered. "There is one, though, who is likely to summon thunder and lightning as soon as I set foot outside, so we should stick to the underground."

"Hey, no argument here!" Alex replied.

"Are you soaked all the way through?" Mia asked.

"No, luckily I had my raincoat on. It's just my hair and my collar. It will dry within the hour," Alex said.

"Okay, as long as you don't get sick, that would really be unfortunate," Mia said.

Alex laughed. "You forget, I'm descended from the Vikings! I have glacier runoff in my veins!"

"And I have ouzo and maple syrup in mine," Mia joked. "So, did you want to stick around, or did you want to get started with the dress shopping?"

"We can hang out here a few more minutes," Alex replied as she removed her soaked scarf and coat. "I thought you might want to know more about what to expect tomorrow evening."

"Ah yes, I was wondering when you'd bring that up."

Alex hailed the bartender. "Two lime margaritas, please. One bill."

Mia smiled, then felt a pang of guilt as she remembered that she never properly libated to the gods for sparing her the interview with the Oracle two days prior.

Ye gods, that was only two days ago. Maybe I'll wait until I have my own place to do a proper libation, otherwise Hester and Ira might get an earful from the neighbours...

"You're not going to pour this gorgeous frozen margarita on the potted plant over there, are you?" Alex asked as she handed a few paper bills to the bartender.

"Not this time, honest!" Mia replied facetiously.

"Good. And try not to do that at the party tomorrow. John is fully cognizant of your body of work so far, and he's fine with it, but still, that might look... odd."

"Understood," Mia replied facetiously. "Wouldn't want to weird out the titans of industry and whatnot!"

"Oh, trust me, that would not be the weirdest thing they'd ever seen... or done, even that day!" Alex said. "Let's grab that table over there. We'll have more privacy," she added, grabbing the margaritas off the counter while tucking her soaked coat and scarf under her elbow.

"Here, let me get those for you," Mia said, taking hold of the drinks. "Does Sotero know that I'm going as your date?"

"Pretty much," Alex answered, draping her garments more elegantly over her arm so as not to soak her flimsy silk blouse. "And before you ask, he's fine with that too."

"So fluffy journalism for a Pagan publication and lesbianism are cool, but not public displays of piety?" Mia asked Alex while following her to a secluded table on the opposite side of the bar.

"Public displays of piety are part of Senator Charles' arsenal to discredit John on the world stage," Alex replied. "I guess you've done a ton of research since Wednesday, in preparation for tomorrow's party?"

"I did, as a matter of fact," Mia replied. "Spent some time in the physics department at McGill to learn more about lunar prospecting and the sorts of things LuNation plans to do once the project launches. It's all fascinating, really. I even read up again on the Moon Treaty, because the last time I skimmed through it back in the aughts was almost exactly thirty pounds ago, when I could fit in a pencil skirt un-ironically."

Alex raised an eyebrow, as a smile crept at the corners of her mouth.

"Gave me a lot more appreciation for the sort of lawyering that you do," Mia continued. "I mean, I already knew about the U.N.'s lofty goals back in the sixties to prohibit the nations of the Earth from staking an ownership claim on the Moon –"

"And other celestial bodies," Alex interrupted jokingly.

"And other celestial bodies," Mia added, "because the exploration of space was supposed to benefit all mankind or some hippie shit like that."

"It was the sixties," Alex said. "And there were superpowers on either side of the Iron Curtain vying for technological supremacy well beyond the bounds of this planet, which is why the U.N. insisted on the peaceful uses of outer space and its related scientific pursuits, for the benefit of all nations, including the developing world. But go on."

"Well, that's pretty much it, isn't it?" Mia replied. "No nation can claim sovereignty on the Moon or other celestial bodies. There, I said it before you did. But that doesn't preclude corporate interests from staking claims for mining and prospecting, even if it's for profit. And all the while I'm here thinking, LuNation is going to make some serious money with lunar mining, even if all that solar energy farming to power their lunar bases will also benefit underserved nations in the southern hemisphere. So my theory is this: Senator Ethan Charles from the great petro-State of hee-haw, is taking exception at Sotero's venture not only for flying under a Canadian flag, but also for threatening to put the fossil fuel industry out of business for good within a decade or so. Does that sound about right?"

Alex nodded a little, her half-concealed smile widening. "You came up with this theory in the last 48 hours?" she asked.

"Pretty much," Mia answered after taking a rather large draught of her half-melted margarita. "An old friend of mine once told me to always follow the money when trying to figure out the root cause of conflict. Good old fear of losing the competitive edge seemed like the most likely explanation for Senator Charles' chicanery."

"Money as the source of all evil?" Alex asked, her gaze fixed upon the centre of her very full glass. "That's a bit cliché, don't you think?"

"Well it's either money, or someone having something that someone else wants but does not have."

"Occam's razor. Your old friend sounds wise," Alex said.

"He has his moments," Mia replied. "Although his choice of spouse makes one question his wisdom."

"Ah," Alex said, as if understanding at last. "How is Phil?"

"He's good."

"Does he suspect the reason behind your line of inquiry?"

"I told him that I'm researching space things for a job... Ow!" Mia said sharply, pinching the bridge of her nose as the brain freeze hit her all at once. "I told him nothing specific, but he did say something a bit freaky that made me question the very fabric of reality for a second or two."

"Oh? Do tell," Alex said before taking a dainty sip of her fully melted drink.

"He said that the Oracle told Willow that I needed to take a break from *Goddess Digest Magazine* to safeguard the Moon for the benefit of all mankind or some crap."

Alex spat out her drink into her little square napkin.

"I told you it was kind of freaky," Mia continued.

"I'll say," Alex agreed.

"The good news is that according to Phil, this is enough to keep Willow off my back for bruising her pride, so we don't have to worry about my former employer running interference."

"I think I'm going to make an appointment with that Oracle lady," Alex mused. "She doesn't seem half as kooky as you paint her out to be."

"Oh, trust me – no I'm not going into it. There is not enough tequila in Montreal to floss my brain after spending all that time interviewing her."

"You might find looking into Senator Charles' history somewhat distasteful as well," Alex said. "Don't get me wrong, you are pretty much on the right track regarding what drives Senator Charles' opposition to John Sotero and the whole LuNation venture, but his methods are, shall we say, rather repugnant. Tomorrow John will meet privately with us during the party, and he and I will brief you more fully on our PR strategy to parry Charles' mudslinging. And as I told you before, your job will be to dig for dirt, and trust me, you will find a lot of it. You might even hit a shallow grave while you're at it. I wanted to tell you this right now, before you meet John, so that you have no misconceptions about what your job will entail."

"What the hell are you saying, Alex?" Mia asked, her heart sinking in her chest. "Are you having second thoughts about me being the right person for the job?"

"Absolutely not," Alex replied. "You are thorough and professional when you are researching information, and you are quite skilled at connecting the dots in ways that others almost never think about. But you're also highly idealistic, and part of me is afraid that you'll fall down a rabbit hole in your never-ending quest to uncover the source of all evil as exemplified in the deeds of unsavoury characters. I just wanted to be sure that you knew what you're getting yourself into."

Mia looked at the remaining dregs of the margarita in her glass and drank the rest. "As I said, I'm in, and I will do what I have to do to see this through to the end," she told Alex as she set down her empty drink on the table

Alex nodded, looking demure yet pleased.

"Now unless you plan on buying me another drink," Mia said finally, "you ought to finish that, so that we can get out of here and buy me a pretty dress."

Alex looked at Mia for a moment, then drained her almost full glass of margarita in one long swallow. Setting down her glass next to Mia's, she said, "Let's."

Mia grabbed her jacket and backpack, making a mental note to keep an eye on Alex lest her petite, slender friend suffer injuries from walking on wobbly stiletto heels after imbibing a full four ounces of eighty-proof alcohol on an empty stomach. As it turned out, Mia's fears were unfounded, for Alessandra DeBeck possessed the sort of near-preternatural resistance to the effects of hard liquor that would have made her Viking ancestors beam with pride, and her Italian forebears weep with dismay.

Chapter Nine

In a twist of fate that would probably have set the Oracle off into a fit of prophetic glee, Saturday fell on the last day of April on the night of the full Moon – a most auspicious time for those of the esoteric persuasion. In days of old, when the scientific and technological understanding of the world of ordinary European people was far less sophisticated than it was today, villagers gathered to light bonfires on May's Eve, or Walpurgis Night, to protect themselves, their crops, and their flocks against witchcraft and evil for the coming year. From the mid-twentieth century onward, the emerging rainbow tide of Earth-worshipping Pagans, Witches, Druids, and other hippies set about to reclaim this folkloric observance as their own, celebrating the coming of the northern summer by dancing round the Maypole and, for some, making whoopee in the woods as their ancestors once did while the fires burned upon the hillsides. Once upon a time, such an assortment of charmed coincidences would also have tickled Mia pink. This evening, however, Mia found herself on the verge of a nervous breakdown, trying with all her might to muster her mettle and not turn into a complete wreck before meeting the powers that be at the LuNation launch party.

It was not because Mia had not prepared for this evening – she spent the entire day at a charming café on the Plateau searching the Web for reputable sources documenting Senator Charles' not-so-secret associations with the fossil fuel industry. If Phil's insights were correct, then Charles' trolling of LuNation's CEO stemmed from his fear of losing a significant portion of his personal wealth once Sotero's array of extraplanetary solar panels went online. Mia also found out through news media articles that Charles' oil empire was at the centre of a great deal of controversy surrounding allegations of abuse and kidnapping of First Nations and Métis women and girls in communities neighbouring oil fields spanning from northern Texas to Alberta, Canada. Mia found the news hard to swallow at first, for surely such accusations would have made headlines in Canada at the very least. This was largely due to the attention garnered by the federal government's neglect of prosecuting the culprits responsible behind the disappearance of literally hundreds of missing and murdered Indigenous women in the last few decades. Mia remembered this very controversy all too well from her brief stint as an office gopher at the Royal Canadian Mounted Police headquarters back in the day, when she was still bright-eyed and bushy-tailed, and believed that she could do her part to save the world by joining Her Majesty's scarlet-clad cowboys. Senator Charles, for his part, remained conveniently and consistently mum on the whole sordid matter, at far as the official public record was concerned.

While Mia delved down the rabbit hole at the café, away from the Greenbaum family home out of respect for her kin as they observed the Sabbath, she somehow managed to remain focused on the task at hand. Sometime between her light lunch and her fourth cup of coffee, she almost felt ready for her impending meeting with the great John Sotero and his wife, Dr. Margaret Richards Sotero, an esteemed scientist and philanthropist in her own right. And yet, as soon as Alex double-parked her sedan on the narrow one-way street to collect her for the evening's festivities, Mia's thoughts began to unravel, leading her to wonder once more whether the past three days had not, in fact, been one long surreal dream. At any moment she would wake up in her old room at Willowdale and get ready for another day's work reporting on the very same rainbow tide of Pagans who likely spent the afternoon enjoying picnics and potlucks and orgies in their high priestess' backyard and whatnot.

When Mia began changing into her new dress in the ladies' room at the launch party venue, she began to fully hyperventilate. Alex suggested, quite judiciously, that she ought to regain her composure by sipping on some wine as soon as they reached the reception hall upstairs. Mia agreed, grateful that her friend remembered the rare instances when the elixir of Dionysus was required to calm her nerves in interesting social situations. Mia was also glad that Alex had insisted on keeping the dress in her car after the epic shopping journey came to an end the previous evening. In hindsight, Mia would have had a terrible time schlepping the garment halfway across the Plateau and hanging it on the back of a chair somewhere, only to see it fall into the last remaining indoor slush puddle in Montreal. Though improbable this late in the season, this scenario remained plausible by virtue of the delayed arrival of this year's spring, as well as the dictates of Murphy pertaining to road salt stains invariably finding their way onto delicate, expensive fabrics.

In his infinite mercy, the benevolent Lord Dionysus saw to it that the lineup for refreshments at the venue's open bar appeared about a half kilometre long, an impressive feat given that the length of the posh, baroque downtown reception hall ran no longer than a full city block. Still, Mia thought it a kindness that she would have to wait for her potion of courage while Alex found them a table. While she stood in line, the servers wasted little time regaling the guests with an endless supply of hors d'oeuvres – all variants of sushi and ornate, exotic garnishes that reminded Mia that she ought to learn more about the finger foods of the world if she ever found the time. After ingesting her eighth California roll and more tempura shrimps than she cared to count, Mia decided it would be wise to wash down the pungent aftertaste of wasabi with tiny vegetable arrangements contained within flimsy shells of dry, salty nori. And yet, just as she thought she had regained a tolerable measure of dignity, a wad of fresh microgreens fell with surgical precision into the cleavage of her brand-new dress as soon as she took a bite of her first veggie burrito.

Ye gods! Can I at least I could get some mileage out of that dress before taking it to the drycleaner?

Mia made a quick spot-check for unseemly stains upon her luxe threads. Luckily for her, no one appeared to take notice of her misadventure, so she promptly fished out the offending greenery from between her ample bosom and tucked it in the napkin she had been holding in her sleeve since the first round of servers came to feed the poor souls still waiting for their spirits in the lineup for the bar.

Okay, no harm done. At least I'm the third next in line. What did Alex say she wanted? Oh right, she didn't. A margarita for her, then. I'll just stick to red wine. Got to keep my wits about me! Where is Alex, anyway?

Mia scanned the vast reception hall for Alex, wondering how long she had been gone putting her clothes from earlier into her car. As she craned her neck to look through the opened doors beyond the lineup to the bar, she saw that the parlour on the other side of the peacock alley at the centre of the venue had just opened its doors.

Right. She's probably out there, mingling with her co-workers. I hope they opened bar stations in the other room because this is ridiculous!

"Madame?" said a young, eager voice behind the bar.

"Wha – oh, right, okay, one red wine and one lime margarita, please," Mia retorted to the barmaid, who looked younger than the already lax

Quebec minimum drinking age – a guideline most Quebeckers thought of more as a suggestion than a law.

"Right away, Madame," said the adolescent alewife.

Before Mia could blink, the girl put a pair of napkins on top the bar, then placed a cup of red wine and a fully mixed glass of margarita at almost the same time, as if conjuring the latter out the aether.

How in the world did she do that? Is this kid some sort of magical alcohol pixie nymph, sent by Dionysus himself to guide me on my path, or just to mess with me?

Mia put such thoughts out of her mind, knowing full well after sharing a home with so many Pagans that questioning seemingly unexplained phenomena when they turned out in one's favour would surely offend the gods, or worse yet, the fae. Mia took a deep, cleansing breath, then grabbed her drinks and tiptoed out of the reception hall in search for Alex. Crossing over into the other, newly opened hall, Mia dodged the influx of guests scrambling to line up at the various bar stations recently set up along the spacious corridor separating the two large parlours. A bartender gave her a bemused look when she evaded a man from slamming squarely into her on his way to acquire his drink. Though Mia almost lost her footing in her four-inch heels, she somehow managed not to spill a single drop of red wine and margarita onto the polished marble floor.

When this is over, I will absolutely have to pour an extra generous libation to the gods and spirits of place. When I get my own apartment, after I get a steady, full-time job. And some plants if my new place doesn't have any trees in the yard, or a yard. Now pull yourself together, you've got this. Investigative research is the one thing you're good at. Even Alex thinks so. And where the hell is Alex?

She found Alex in the second parlour, at the centre of an empty dance floor around which lavishly decorated tables and chairs had been set up for the evening meal. Despite looking gorgeous and radiant as always, Alex appeared rather miffed, in the way that women usually do when made to endure unwanted attention from male admirers while also trying to keep the appearance of politeness for propriety's sake. Mia quickly detected the source of Alex's exasperation; next to her a young man stood, clearly trying to hold her attention with incessant chatter, and oblivious to her annoyance. For a fleeting moment, Mia pitied the chap, for he could not know that the lithe, pretty lady with the perfectly coiffed hair and flawless skin was immune to the charms of men. And yet, Mia could not help but admire the lad's determination, as if redoubling his efforts to hold Alex's attention could override his quarry's sexual proclivity, which was encoded in her DNA since long before her parents were born.

Rallying as much piety as was possible amidst a crowd of strangers, Mia raised her cup of red wine and drained it in three swallows, imagining herself drawing down the essence of chivalry into her very bones. Evidently, the medicine's anticipated effects would prove very much diminished by the vast quantities of sushi she recently ingested. Still, Mia would not allow such an insignificant thing as biology deter her in her quest to fend off Alex's nuisance. Just as she squared her shoulders and set her sights towards the centre of the dining parlour, a server handed her another full cup of red wine and winked at her before disappearing in the throng.

I shall rescue thee, fair maiden. The gods are with me. That boy never had a chance...

Confident that the gods would protect her booze from falling upon the ground, Mia sped to the centre of the room, her reptilian brain giddy in anticipation for battle.

You were supposed to draw down the spirit of chivalry, not the god of war! Calm your tits, now is not the time to start a brawl, not when your future career is at stake.

Mia slowed down as she drew near Alex and the young man, affecting an innocent look for good measure. To her surprise, the lad turned to glance at Mia when he saw Alex's line of sight shifting in her direction.

"I see you brought a friend," he said in a suave, smarmy tone that made Mia clench her fists.

Don't crush the glasses. This guy is not worth the stitches.

"Hi sweetie," Mia said sanguinely as she handed Alex her drink. Turning her attention towards the young man, she said, "Hello, I'm Mia. I see you met my wife."

The boy stared at Mia, a sly smile upon his lips.

"And you are?" Mia continued, extending her hand formally.

"Brian Woodhead," he said, flipping a business card from his pocket and handing it to Mia instead of shaking her hand. "Charmed."

Mia grabbed the card with her proffered hand and took a quick peek. "So, you're an intern at a law firm?" she asked the lad who seemed far too young to hold an undergraduate degree.

Ye gods, why is everyone so young? Maybe I'm getting old…

"No, I'm a lawyer," Woodhead answered with an uncomfortable laugh. "Just like the lovely Ms. DeBeck. We were just talking shop."

Alex raised her eyebrows and shook her head slightly when she realized that Woodhead was still looking at Mia.

"I didn't know there were so many space law specialists in Montreal," Mia said, staring down the lad with a fierce glower.

"Oh, I'm not –"

Woodhead paused, his gaze set about three feet behind Mia's left shoulder. He blanched almost imperceptibly, though Mia definitely noticed his fright.

"Excuse me, ladies," Woodhead said, quickly grabbing another business card from his pocket and hastily handing it to Alex before escaping into the gathering crowd.

"John! Maggie! Thank god!" Alex told the people who were obviously standing behind Mia.

Mia turned around and saw the great John Sotero himself, drink in hand, accompanied by a handsome, elegant woman she assumed to be Dr. Margaret Richards Sotero, also drink in hand.

"You must be Ms. Thorne," said the woman, a wide smile upon her comely face.

Mia nodded, momentarily at a loss for words.

"John, Maggie, this is my friend Mia," Alex said. "Mia, this is John Sotero."

"Hi", Mia said, shaking John Sotero's hand.

"Call me John."

"And Dr. Margaret Sotero," Alex continued.

"Call me Maggie, please," the good doctor told Mia as she also shook her hand.

"You looked like you were in need of rescue from that guy," John told Alex. "But Ms. Thorne –"

"It's Mia, please," Mia interrupted.

"Before Mia beat us to it," John continued with good humour.

"From the look of your body language," Maggie told Mia, "you looked like you were about to tear him limb from limb!"

"Yeah, I don't like to pull the cliché angry lesbian lover act," Mia replied. "But under the circumstances it seemed like the right thing to do. Who the hell was that guy anyway?"

"He said he was headhunting for his employer," Alex answered, "but I know every law firm and lawyer from here to Toronto. This guy was a phony."

"One of Senator Charles' lackeys," Mia asked, verbalizing a thought that seemingly came out of nowhere.

"Could be," John replied. "It wouldn't be the first time his camp tried to sabotage me by poaching my best talent. But we'll talk about this more after dinner. Shall we take our seats?"

"Uh –" Mia stammered.

"You and Alex will be sitting at our table, dear," Maggie declared benevolently.

Mia nodded, following Alex and the Soteros to the head table at the centre of the main wall. The lights dimmed on cue, and an artist's rendering of John Sotero's iconic *Aries I* shuttle landing next to the prospective LuNation solar panel farm on the Moon came into full view onto the huge projection screen above the head table. Mia bit her lip, recognizing the very same image she saw on a pamphlet in Alex's car only three days ago.

Okay, things just got real. I guess this means it's showtime!

Marisol Charbonneau

Chapter Ten

The evening's proceedings turned out exactly as one could expect from a gala celebrating the launch of a resource exploitation venture bound for the Moon. During the dinner service the guests were entertained by the obligatory speeches from various dignitaries, including a few representatives from the provincial and federal governments, as well as from members of various international space exploration agencies. The Canadian Space Agency was there as well as NASA, the European Space Agency, JAXA and the CNSA representing Japan and China, respectively, the BSA from John Sotero's native Brazil, and others. Naturally as CEO, John gave a speech thanking everyone for coming to the event, offered a few encouraging words with regards to funding and projected revenue, and provided the expected timeline for the solar generation branch of LuNation to come online. He also briefly mentioned his wife's trailblazing work on adapting lunar habitats to allow for the peculiarities of human physiology in reduced gravity environments – something that promised to set a precedent for off-world exploration and colonization protocols for decades to come.

As John praised Maggie's work, he remained tantalizingly vague with the specifics of said protocols. Alex probably noticed the maddening effect this had on Mia, as she whispered to her at the end of John's allocution, "Keep this in mind when we talk with them later.'

When Mia answered Alex with a slightly peeved look, Maggie smiled at them both and said, "We will explain everything, I promise."

It took another hour and a half until dinner finally concluded, after which the guests were welcomed to join in the compulsory and gloriously awkward dance party in which all the songs were Moon themed. About three songs into the playlist, Alex had to scold Mia for chuckling like a tween girl who just heard a dirty joke for the first time.

"What?" Mia retorted as the fourth song began playing. "I told you! I wasn't the only who thought that LuNation would turn the Moon into a giant disco ball in a few decades once it's entirely covered with solar panels. The DJ gets it!"

"We're not quite there yet," John said, returning to the head table. Looking at Alex and Maggie, he gave the two a small nod and turned his gaze straight towards Mia. "Shall we adjourn our discussion in the salon?" he said while proffering his arm to his wife.

"Let's," Maggie answered, picking up her purse and taking John's arm.

Mia thought the gesture sweet in its gallantry, even though she figured by this point that Maggie did not need her husband to steady her or lead her, either figuratively or otherwise. As for John, Mia found that he was even more magnanimous than he imagined him to be in person, without an iota of pretence despite his impressive achievements in his professional endeavours. After spending only a few hours and an elaborate meal with the Soteros, Mia decided that she would accept any assignment they would give her, so that she could contribute to the success of LuNation Mining International, and to the triumph of humanity over its addiction to fossil fuels.

"So, Mia," John said after the four of them settled behind closed doors of a private den at the end of the venue's gilded hallway. "I know Alex gave you very little information to go on with regards to my run-ins with Senator Ethan Charles – you need to understand, she was only following my instructions. I know for a fact that she wanted to tell you more, but I asked her not to at the time. So, given the limited info you had, why do you think Senator Charles has it in for me and the work that I do?"

Mia took a slow, deliberate sip from the mostly full cup of wine she had brought with her.

"I think it's pretty obvious," she said after a brief pause. "Charles is significantly invested in Big Oil and the natural gas industry. Your – I mean, LuNation's solar energy farming is a threat to his wealth and the livelihood of many of his richest backers. Evidently, his so-called crusade or whatever is nothing more than a smear campaign meant to sabotage your investment prospects, so that he and his oil baron buddies can continue funding their lavish lifestyle by poisoning the Earth for profit."

"So you think this is about money?" Maggie asked, her tone strangely wistful.

"Well, yes," Mia answered, confused by Maggie's question. She looked at Alex, hoping to read her friend's countenance for a clue as to Maggie's inquiry, but Alex's gaze was fixed on John. Shifting her focus to the Soteros, Mia saw Maggie and John exchange silent nods and knowing looks. Mia bit her lip, wondering if she had inadvertently said something stupid.

"You are not wrong," John said after an unbearably tense moment. "At the beginning, Charles went through a lot of effort framing his objections to our work in terms of a capitalist crisis, claiming that free solar energy would take away jobs from his constituents. But recently he's shifted gears by aligning his interests with those of the Evangelical Right. Do you have any idea why?"

"The kind of people who repeatedly vote against their own interests are those most likely to be religious," Mia answered. "They tend to be poor and uneducated and are afraid of change because it's an unknown. A threat. Because it makes them feel vulnerable and unprepared for the future, so they do what people have always done – they find a scapegoat. Whether it's a group of people, a hostile nation, or even just an idea, then they get panicky and lose their minds, and then innocent people get hurt. I mean, in the early modern period, there were the witch hunts in Europe when thousands of people were murdered for absolutely no reason. In the nineteen-fifties they were hunting communists in America and in the eighties there was the bogus Satanic Panic, where people actually went to jail for absolutely no reason. And now we have the –" Mia pondered her words for a moment. "The Technological Terror? I think it's an accurate enough term for Charles' particular brand of attempted *fuckwittage*, pardon my French."

John smiled but said nothing.

"Are you telling me there's something else I'm missing?" Mia asked at last, her nerves beginning to fray at the Soteros' reticence.

"Like John said," Maggie replied, "your insights are correct, as far as Ethan's supporters are concerned."

Ethan? Are we all buddies now?

"The look on your face just confirmed my suspicions," Maggie continued. "You see, Ethan – Senator Charles – has been very careful not to expose his past relationship with us. And by us, I mean myself, specifically. You see, Ethan Charles is my ex-husband."

Mia's eyebrows receded all the way to her hairline. "Oh?" she muttered weakly, feeling as though she committed a cardinal sin by not uncovering this rather interesting tidbit during her hours of research. She looked at Alex, who answered with a sympathetic look.

"So it's jealousy," Mia added, shifting uncomfortably on the overly firm and mostly decorative sofa.

"Yes, and no," Maggie said. "It's more complicated than that. Oh dear, where should I even begin?"

"Your research," Alex interjected. "We can start with that."

"Right," Maggie replied. "To make a long story short, I married Ethan back when I was still a pre-med student. Ethan was heir to an oil conglomerate, but you already knew that. He was born into money, and wanted to keep his place among the one percent, no matter the cost. Meanwhile I wanted to go into med school to help improve the human condition. You can see where this story's headed. One time during a dinner party with his industry friends and business associates, I brought up the subject of divesting their vast wealth from fossil fuels due to the negative impact of greenhouse gasses on human and planetary health. Mind you, I was very young and naïve when that happened, but that did not excuse the way Ethan reacted. He flew into a rage and humiliated me in front of all our friends. I was so disgusted by his behaviour that I left him that very night and filed for divorce.

"My parents were appalled that I'd left him – especially my mother who hoped that I would turn out like her, a social climber. So I left and I continued my studies, specializing in space medicine instead of withering away in a mansion somewhere as some rich asshole's trophy wife. Years later, long before we became an item, John recruited me straight from NASA's Jet Propulsion Laboratory for some research I had previously conducted on the long-term effects of microgravity on human physiology. Shortly after I relocated to Quebec to work with John in his start-up, Ethan showed up, drunk as a skunk, to claim that all my work belonged to him since his alimony payments funded my studies."

Mia spat out her sip of wine. Alex produced a wad of napkins seemingly out of thin air and handed it to Mia. Surprisingly, the wine had disappeared into the aether somehow, for no trace of the expelled elixir remained on the white carpet and couches.

"Wait until you hear what happened next," Alex said, a smile creeping upon her lips.

"I called the RCMP and had him deported," John added. "He's been on a Canadian no-fly list since."

"I never read about that!" Mia said, trying hard to suppress a chuckle while her eyes continued to look for her boozy spittle. "You'd think something like that would make the news!"

"That was years ago, before Ethan went into politics," Maggie answered. "As you can imagine, he's been following my career with, shall we say, great interest. Recently, many of my colleagues and former collaborators published the results of their own studies on the long-term effects of microgravity on the human body, and their conclusions corroborated my own. What we found was that women tend to fare better in space in the long term. For reasons we are still trying to figure out, women suffer fewer ill effects from prolonged exposure to microgravity as men do. This informed John's decision to staff the first generation of LuNation's off-world bases with mostly female staff, with planned twelve-month rotations to relieve the first waves of builders and engineers from developing space sickness."

"Now Mia, can you imagine how Senator Charles took the news once he got word of our plans to staff our lunar bases with mostly women?" John asked.

"I bet he threw a tantrum," Mia answered, understanding at last the scope of the task that lay ahead of her. "So many things make sense now, in a horrible sort of way. But how did he find out? Your decision to staff the lunar bases with mostly women was not exactly front-page news, and it wasn't mentioned anywhere on the corporate website either. I read it almost in its entirety not even two days ago!"

"We know," Alex said. "I told John and Maggie that you would have done your due diligence before tonight."

"No, we're not going advertise all the details of our staffing plans to the press just yet," John said. "We wanted to wait until our initial construction crews were already on their way to the landing site. The first wave of builders will include men, of course, but we didn't want to make any press releases as to our long-term roster just yet in case it raised any controversies with the MRA crowd and whatnot."

"You mean those wags who are most likely to cry gender discrimination whenever women get a break, even though women have been historically barred from going to space in the West until the eighties?" Mia asked with some measure of sarcasm.

"The very same," John answered with a nod.

"People like Senator Charles, who's not exactly known for his enlightened views towards women from what I gathered," Mia added.

"Exactly," Maggie replied. "So now you understand how Ethan might have felt personally attacked by our plan to send a largely female crew on the Moon. You can imagine how this could have offended his already egregiously misogynistic sensibilities, and the fact that it came from me probably triggered him in a way he never thought possible."

"That's the reason why we're thinking he decided to align himself with the Religious Far Right in the United States," Alex added. "He wants vocal allies in his smear campaign to discredit John and Maggie's ground-breaking staffing decisions. He wants to make it look like a moral issue with the ultra-conservative, anti-feminist Talibangelicals instead of what it truly is – a petty personal vendetta. And that's where you come in."

"So you *do* want me to write a piece about Senator Charles to expose what a piece of shit he is," Mia said.

"It's not as simple as that," John replied. "We need you to find irrefutable evidence that our assumptions about his motivations are correct and expose them in such a way that he can't spin it in his favour."

"That's the difficult part," Maggie said. "Such things will not be easy to prove. Ethan might appear indiscreet in all aspects of his personal life, but if there's one thing he's good at, it's hiring people to make his vices look like virtues."

"I've got to say," Mia added, "I might not think much about the man, but whoever gave him the idea to court the Religious Reich was probably a genius. What he's doing should be illegal, but unfortunately the U.S. doesn't have the same laws that we have on hate speech. His new friends are essentially a cult with way too much political power, and they almost never let such pesky things like the facts change their minds about anything."

"So, given the difficulty of the assignment we're proposing," Maggie said, "we would completely understand if you declined our offer. Alex?"

Taking her cue from Maggie, Alex grabbed her briefcase off a low table by the couch where Mia sat and produced a white paper folder, then handed the item to Mia.

Mia glimpsed the document, until Alex turned the first page and pointed at a dollar amount with her perfectly manicured finger.

"This is the retainer we're offering for your services," she told Mia. "You will also have access to a discretionary expense account and LuNation's legal counsel at your disposal. That means me. The rest of the document is your standard non-disclosure agreement. Take the time to read through, you don't have to sign right away."

Mia nodded. "I'll read it right now if you don't mind," she answered.

"That's fine with us," John said. "And if you have any questions –"

"Nope, it's all fine," Mia interrupted as she took a pen from her clutch and signed her name on the dotted line.

"Okay, then," Alex said, handing the document to John for his signature. "We will send you a picture scan of the offer for your files tonight and give you a copy if you'd like when you come to our offices on Monday morning. We'll have HR send you the onboarding email first thing tomorrow morning."

"Welcome to the team," Maggie said finally, giving Mia a warm, maternal smile.

"Cheers!" Mia answered with a polite nod, before draining the rest of her wine in one swallow.

And now for the fun part, to root out the source of all evil.

Marisol Charbonneau

Chapter Eleven

"Are you sure you're okay?" Alex asked Mia as they walked towards Alex's car in the underground parking garage.

"I'm fine!" Mia answered in a tone that suggested she was definitely not fine.

"I saw the signs, Mia. The conversation was upsetting you, especially the part about the Senator's rampant misogyny. Are you sure you don't want to withdraw? You still can, John and Maggie won't hold it against you!"

"NO! I'm doing this!" Mia yelled out. "Alex... he can't get away with this! It's fuckheads like him that are the reason why some men feel that they have the right to silence women by threatening a 'Montreal-style massacre' whenever they lose arguments on the Internet! Do you know where that expression comes from? Or were you too young to remember the *École Polytechnique* massacre in 1989? That was the reason why my dad changed our family name when I was a kid. We happened to share a last name with the gunman, so my dad *anglicized* our name out of outrage!"

"Mia," Alex said, "I know. I'm so sorry –"

"For what? The indignity of going through the Francophone school system in the nineties with an Anglo surname? He was never the most stable type, my dad, but here we are."

"Look, we shouldn't talk about this here."

"Why not? Because that guy from earlier, Brian what's-his-face, might overhear us? I hope he shows himself, because I'd –"

"Yes, I know," Alex said soothingly. "Please, we can talk about it more in the car. Here, hold on."

Alex pulled out the key remote from her coat pocket and unlocked her sedan. Mia clumsily climbed aboard and pulled out a tissue from her clutch.

"It's just allergies," she told Alex as she began to dab her eyes.

"Right. Allergies in an indoor parking lot."

"It's spring!" Mia protested.

"We're surrounded by concrete, and we're barely out of mud-and-flood season, Mia. Spring doesn't begin until next week. Look, let's talk about this. You're going to need some kind of strategy, legally speaking. As you said, Charles isn't doing anything illegal, and some of his followers might even praise him for his current course of action."

"We need an Operation Mindfuck," Mia said sullenly.

"Say again?"

"Operation Mindfuck, whereby one fucks with another's mind in order to defeat them? It's a Discordian thing. You heard about the Discordians, right?"

Alex answered Mia with a blank stare.

"Of course you haven't," Mia replied, as if talking to herself. "You don't run in those circles."

"Aren't they like those eco-friendly, socially conscious, activist Satanists, but with ADHD?" Alex asked with the most neutral expression she could muster.

Now it was Mia's turn to answer with a vapid stare, until she burst into a fit of cathartic laughter. "Oh, my, gods," she said once she caught her breath. "I needed that!"

"So, you were saying about Discordians?"

"This is one of those types of situations where I wished I was still at Willowdale," Mia said. "Don't get me wrong, I'm not withdrawing from the LuNation assignment. It's just that Allen would know exactly what to do in terms of mind-fuckery right now. So would Erinna, but that's because the girl is pure chaos wrapped in a hoodie and topped with a mop of purple hair –"

"Call them," Alex interrupted Mia suddenly.

"The local chapter of the Temple of Eris is closed right now," Mia replied. "Don't ask me how I know. Yeah, it's weird that a bunch of people who worship the Goddess of chaos, confusion, and strife should keep regular business hours, but this is a weird world we live in. And no, I'm not saying that because they're located at Willowdale – they're not. Their headquarters are in a converted ice cream van that belongs to this guy I know from Concordia back in the day, Dennis something, though now he officially goes by the name Horkos –"

"No," Alex interrupted again. "Call Allen and Erinna, your friends at Willowdale."

"Are you serious? What about the NDA?"

"As long as you remain vague and discreet, there is nothing barring you from consulting third parties. I have a stack of NDAs in my briefcase. As long as they agree to sign one each, you're in the clear, legally speaking."

Mia blinked a few times, allowing Alex's words to sink in. Once her mental buffering ran its course, Mia fished her phone out of her clutch and hit the speed dial for Allen's number. She took a few calming breaths as the phone rang twice on the other end.

"He's not answering," she told Alex nervously, until a familiar voice responded.

"Just breathe," Alex said.

"Hi Allen, it's me," Mia said at last in a tone that betrayed her remorse for not calling him sooner. "I'm good. I'm really sorry for being incommunicado for the past couple of days. That was pretty shitty of me, but I hope you understand that things gave been a bit insane on my end. Yeah, that's why I'm calling. I need to talk to you and Erinna… and maybe also Phil. Okay, here's the deal: Can you three meet me for brunch tomorrow? You know that place by the giant orange julip near the 15? That big orange blob you can see in satellite pictures of the island, where the Illuminati meet every month? Yeah, it's got free parking. Do you know Dennis? Discordian Dennis? Yeah, Tin Foil Hat Dennis. That's the place where he always parks his van even though he doesn't work there. Look, I can't really get into it right now. Alex is driving me to my sister's. Yeah, *that* Alex. *Space balls* Alex –"

Mia turned her gaze towards Alex and mouthed the words "I'll explain later," while Allen pontificated loudly with what any reasonable person would have construed as an expletive-laden tirade.

"Okay, see you guys tomorrow at ten-thirty, then?" Mia told him at last. "What's that? Sure, Othmane can come too, why not? Okay, see you tomorrow. Give my love to everyone! Bye."

Alex took hold of Mia's hand.

"Don't worry," Mia said absentmindedly. "It's nothing personal. He uses the word 'motherfucker' a lot. He's a sweetheart, really, he's just protective of his friends."

"I wasn't worried about him," Alex answered with a soft chuckle. "I'm more concerned about you. You can crash at my place in one of my guest bedrooms if you'd like. I've got your change of clothes in the trunk if that makes you feel better."

"No, but thanks," Mia answered. "I should get home. I need to think."

"Okay," Alex acquiesced, starting the engine and pulling the sedan out of the underground parking garage.

Chapter Twelve

Alex drove halfway across the city-island by way of the tranquil Chemin Camilien-Houde, a mountain road that conveniently sidestepped the legendary Saturday night traffic in Montreal. Now that the mud-and-flood season finally surrendered to proper boreal spring, Alex took great care to avoid the roadside potholes as well as the deluge of late-night partygoers eager to leave the comfort of their overheated dwellings and ring in the merry morning of May. Within a span of twenty minutes, Mia was at the curbside of the Greenbaum family home in Outremont, geographically close yet worlds away from the city's notoriously mirthful downtown and Plateau areas.

For some reason, the living room lights were still turned on, even though it was well past midnight, and the entirety of the household, teenagers and all, should have dutifully gone to bed. Had Hester kept the lights on for her houseguest to find her way home? Mia smiled, her heart swelling with gratitude for her older sister's forbearance. Her delight was short-lived, for she quickly noticed a familiar VW Minibus parked across the street. Her curiosity piqued, Mia looked at Alex, who appeared not to take notice of the crown jewel of the Willowdale fleet parked across the street from the Greenbaum home.

"Hold on a minute," Mia said, exiting Alex's car with great haste.

"What? Is everything okay?" Alex replied frantically, following Mia into the chilly early spring night.

"We've got Pagans!" Mia answered. "And they're not in the car!"

"Mia, wait!" Alex cried out. "You forgot your clothes in the trunk!"

"That's okay, I'll get them in a bit," Mia replied. "Fuckery is afoot!"

Alex sighed, as she often did whenever Mia partook too much of the grape. She grabbed her purse and exited her parked sedan, taking great care to shut off the engine and making sure that her parking spot was legal for the time being. Meanwhile, Mia grabbed her own keys and opened the door to Hester's house.

"You'll have to be quiet," Mia said in a low voice. "My family is asleep."

"Okay, sure," Alex replied. "Do you need a glass of water or something? You had, like, seven cups of wine before we left."

"One for each deadly sin!" Mia retorted facetiously. "But seriously though, I'll just take a look... What the –"

"And there she is!" Hester said as Mia stepped into the vestibule, with Alex at her heel.

"You guys waited up?" Mia asked nervously. "I told you this party might end in the wee hours."

"Oh, this party is only getting started," Mia heard Ira say with a soft laugh.

Mia paused. Though preternaturally hale for his age, Ira Greenbaum always went to bed before ten o'clock every night, especially on the Sabbath, when he and Hester would perform their conjugal duties – a mitzvah according to Rabbinic tradition.

Oh dear gods, what is going on in there?

"Um, hey," Mia replied anxiously, like a teenager caught sneaking back home after curfew. "My friend Alex drove me home. She just needs to use the washroom –"

"Alex!" Hester exclaimed happily. "Come on in! I haven't seen you in years!"

"Hello," Alex said politely, poking her head out of the vestibule while Mia removed her shoes and stepped inside the living room.

As Mia suspected, Hester and Ira were not alone; the four younger Greenbaum children, Daniel, Ariel, Ruthie and Moshe, stood behind the sofas where Allen, Erinna, Othmane, and Mary Jane sat.

"Mary Jane?" Mia whispered absentmindedly, surprised at finding the ex-novitiate she barely knew in the Greenbaums' living room.

"Hi Mia," Mary Jane replied timidly. "And you must be Alex?"

Alex waved at the Greenbaums and the others, not sure what to say by way of introductions. Hester rose to her feet and gave Alex a hug, which Alex reciprocated awkwardly.

"Would you like some tea?" Hester asked warmly. "Ruthie, Moshe, get our guests another pot of tea and some cookies."

The two youngest Greenbaums followed Hester into the kitchen while Ira nodded politely to Alex who did the same, well aware of orthodox Jewish men's prohibition against shaking the hands of women who are not close relatives. Mia artlessly introduced Alex to the remaining Greenbaum boys and the denizens of Willowdale, still confused as to Mary Jane's presence at this gathering. She did notice Phil's absence, though it made perfect sense to Mia that Phil would abstain from darkening the door of his ex-wife home.

"What the heck is going on?" Mia asked finally.

"Your friends are staging an intervention," Ira answered, stifling a laugh.

"We need to talk," Allen said.

"Couldn't this wait until brunch tomorrow?" Mia replied incredulously. "How long have you been waiting here anyway?"

"About five minutes," Erinna answered. "We literally got here just before you did."

"Why?" Mia asked sharply, her patience wearing thin.

"We know about your new job, baby girl," Allen said.

Mia almost uttered a string of profanities but held back out of consideration for the pious Greenbaums present.

"Did Phil tell you what I was up to?" Mia asked exasperatedly.

"Actually no," Allen replied. "It was Katie. She saw you and Phil on campus Thursday and snuck out of school to follow you."

"She also saw you the next day with your lady friend," Othmane added, "and followed you into the Queen Elizabeth and a few other dress shops."

Mia gasped, looking straight at Alex with a look of alarm.

"I didn't see her either," Alex said, raising an eyebrow.

"Did her mother ask her to spy on me!?" Mia shrieked.

"No, we did," Allen answered.

"When the school noticed Katie was gone on Thursday," Erinna said, "they called her mom at the office, and of course I answered first, and then by the time Willow found out and went over there, Katie had snuck back in the school so they said never mind, and that was that."

"The kid has a career ahead of her in surveillance or espionage!" Alex said admiringly.

"So when Katie got home," Erinna continued, "she confronted Phil about your meeting. He told her that he suspected you might have gotten yourself involved into some weird investigation concerning a powerful politician's motives for opposing lunar mining and prospecting. Allen and I overheard, and we added two and two together since you'd spent time with Alex on Wednesday, and she specializes in space law. We also overheard Phil mention to Katie that you would be in his office all day on Friday to do some research. Allen did due diligence on Alex while Othmane researched all that he could on Alex's employer. We found the controversy started by that Senator Charles fellow. The results were, let's just say, somewhat troubling, so we got Mary Jane to help out researching Senator Charles."

Mia looked again at Mary Jane, still confused as to how or why she got recruited into this peculiar situation.

"I used to do tech support at the convent back in the day," Mary Jane answered Mia's quizzical stare. "I was the... tech nun, if you will."

"Yeah, so when you called me, I gathered the troops and we headed straight here, thinking you might be in trouble," Allen chimed in. "You might not know it yet, but you are in way over your head, baby girl."

"Excuse me," Alex said diplomatically. "I can assure you that my employer is taking every precaution –"

"I'm sure you think that John Sotero will hire a crew of retired green berets to protect Mia, *Alex*," Allen replied curtly. "Because that's pretty much what you'll need against that whack job you're having her investigate!"

"All right, everyone calm down!" Ira said as Hester returned to the living room carrying a full teapot, with Ruthie and Moshe following closely behind with plates of crackers and cheeses and crudités.

"Mia, what in God's name have you gotten yourself into?" Hester asked, having obviously heard the last part of the conversation.

"I'm not in trouble, guys." Mia sighed. She looked at Alex.

"The cat is already out of the bag," Alex answered with a shrug. "Just wait until I get the NDAs in the car before you say anything too specific."

"Daniel, go with her," Ira told his son. "Moshe, Ruthie, Ariel, go to bed. That's enough excitement for tonight." Turning his attention to Mia, he said, "whatever this is about, please keep it down. Hester and I are going to bed."

Mia nodded. "Sorry about this, Ira, Hester," she whispered. "We'll make this brief."

"No, take your time," Ira replied, placing his arm in the small of Hester's back and prompting her to go upstairs.

Mia smiled, immediately understanding his meaning. She waited until Alex and Daniel returned with Alex's briefcase, then took a seat on Ira's armchair.

"Okay here's the thing," she told the denizens of Willowdale once Daniel had gone upstairs to retire for the night. "If I tell you what's really going on, all of you will need to sign an NDA because what I'm about to tell you might cause a lot of embarrassment to the Soteros. They're the ones who run LuNation, but I guess you already know that by now. And also because I really need your help. Especially you," Mia added, turning her gaze to Allen.

"We have your back," Allen said.

"Yeah, we're here for you," Erinna added, to which Othmane and Mary Jane nodded in agreement.

Alex pulled out a stack of NDAs from her briefcase and handed Allen the first copy. She produced a pen and handed it to him. Allen signed his copy, then looked up at Mia. "What kind of help do you need?" he asked her.

"We need to talk about Operation Mindfuck," Mia answered, to which Erinna squealed in delight. Othmane and Mary Jane exchanged confused looks.

"I was waiting for you to say that," Allen said with a grin.

Chapter Thirteen

"Okay," Mia said after Erinna, Othmane, and Mary Jane finished signing their own NDAs. "Your instincts were correct about John Sotero hiring me to investigate Senator Ethan Charles to get him to back off from his crusade against LuNation. And I am touched that you all came here tonight to make sure I was okay. Seriously guys, that was really sweet, though maybe showing up at my sister's house this late at night, especially after the family just finished observing the Sabbath, might have been a bit much. But just so you know, Senator Charles has no idea I even exist, except perhaps as Alex's fake wife, if that barely shaving lad at the party really was one of his minions."

Mia rummaged through her clutch and grabbed the business card the young man gave her earlier that evening. "This is his card, if you also want to check him out," she continued, handing the business card to Allen. "He tried to headhunt Alex tonight, right at the LuNation launch. He had some brass balls, I'll give him that. He didn't even flinch when I put on my angry lesbian face!"

Allen threw a quick glance at the card, then passed it over to Erinna who showed it to Othmane and Mary Jane.

"We can run a quick check on this clown," Allen said, as Mary Jane placed the card on the low coffee table and removed her laptop from her satchel.

"Alex thinks he might be assuming the identity of a lawyer just to mess with us," Mia added. "Anyway, he left before things got weird. And they absolutely got weird. So here's the thing: Senator Charles might be a whack job, but he has brilliantly courted the Christian Far Right in the United States and manipulated the media to make his beef against Sotero and the whole LuNation enterprise look like a moral issue."

"But why?" Erinna asked. "What the hell?"

"What the hell indeed," Mia agreed. "So get a load of this: it's not exactly a state secret that Charles is a raging misogynist, right? Well, today I learned that his whole jihad is driven by the fact that he found out, and we're still not quite sure how, that LuNation's mining bases will be staffed mostly by women. Maggie, I mean Dr. Margaret Richards Sotero, who happens to be married to *that* Mr. Sotero, co-wrote one of many studies that confirm that women do better long-term in space, health-wise. That rubbed Charles the wrong way because, you know, the part about him being a male chauvinist pig."

Allen, Erinna, Othmane, and Mary Jane stared at Mia unblinkingly, while Alex bit her lip.

"That's pretty fucked up," Erinna said.

"I told you he was a whack job," Allen agreed.

"But wait... there's more," Mia continued. "Dr. Margaret Richards Sotero also happens to be Ethan Charles' ex-wife. So there's that, too. And here we are."

"John and Maggie Sotero asked Mia to investigate Senator Charles to find a way to expose his true motives to the world at large," Alex said. "And by that we mean, specifically, his opposition to a major part of LuNation's future off-world roster being women, not the part about him being Maggie's ex-husband. My job, for the near future, is to make sure Mia is legally protected, in case Charles comes after her with accusations of libel and the like."

"Wow," Allen said.

"I know," Mia replied. "And as you can imagine, since Charles got in bed with the uber-religious Far Right, exposing his misogyny to fellow misogynists will not exactly make him lose points in the polls –"

"So why did you take the job, Mia?" Othman asked earnestly. "This seems like one of those scenarios where you're damned if you do, and damned if you don't!"

"Because I was sick and tired of Willow condescending to me and I wanted a job that presented a real challenge, for once," Mia answered sincerely, if a little bit bitingly due to her creeping exhaustion. "Because I wanted to prove that I was a real journalist, not some middle-aged fuck-up who can't get her shit together, personally and professionally. I wanted to finally do what I was meant to do: expose bad actors so that they can be stopped, otherwise I'd be no better than human sheep who prefer to stay home and do nothing, and through inaction become complicit in their own fleecing. But now, I think you might have been right about me being in over my head, because I see no other way through this than –"

"Operation Mindfuck," Allen said calmly, in a way one would expect from an urban yogi.

"Yeah, so figuring this out was the hard part; now the easy part is to figure out *how* to effectively fuck with his mind," Mia said.

"How do you fuck with a man like Senator Ethan Charles?" Allen asked. "A man whose strength lies in appealing to a bunch of bat-shit Christo-fascist knuckle-draggers..."

"By going after his mom?" Othmane jested.

"No, sweetie, that's been done," Mary Jane said, startling Mia, who had already forgotten that she was there in the first place.

So Othmane and Mary Jane are dating. Wait a minute, does Othmane actually think the ex-novitiate is still a virgin?

"And no one," Mary Jane continued while typing furiously at her laptop, "living or dead, will ever top the lampooning of that hateful church leader... You know, the one whose congregation routinely picketed soldiers' funerals because of gays in the military? Yeah him. He got trolled by a performance arts collective who turned his mother into a lesbian posthumously."

And there she is. Sister Mary Punk-Rock-Rebel, praising the methods of chaos-mongering altruists who clean highways while wearing hooded black capes and wielding pitchforks.

Ah, Othmane, you truly are too pure for this world.

"Oooh! I know!" Erinna blurted out excitedly. "We can take his garden variety, basic batshit crazy and make it look like he's propelled it into the stratosphere! We can make him look so insane that even his literal, goddamn Nazi allies will disown him! No, hear me out, if he's so butthurt by the idea of women having actual important jobs on Moon bases, then maybe we can make him look like he'd want to blow up the Moon if LuNation carries out its plans!"

"Blowing up the Moon?" Mia asked, slightly amused despite her weariness. "I admit, that's very, *creative*, but no nation on Earth, not even the U.S., has that kind of arsenal."

"But he has resources –" Erinna added.

"Wait a minute," Mia interrupted, as if receiving a spark of momentary divine inspiration. "If he's made to look *obsessed* with the Moon and with women *being* on the Moon, and whatnot, we could make him look as though he would use his vast wealth to, I don't know, not blow it up, but rather restore it to its original conditions, as per Scripture?"

Alex, Allen, Erinna, Othmane and Mary Jane all gave Mia a blank look.

"Err, what?" Othmane muttered.

"No, Mia's on to something," Mary Jane said. "I remember reading passages in the Gospel of Mark where it was mentioned that after the arrival of the Son of Man, the sun will be darkened, the Moon shall not give its light, and the stars will fall from the heavens…"

"You're forgetting the Books of Jeremiah and Deuteronomy where God threatened to punish His people for worshipping the Moon," said a young Greenbaum from the landing of the stairs.

"Moshe," Mia exclaimed. "I though you'd gone to bed!"

"I did," Moshe replied. "My bedroom is right next to my parents'. I'm a light sleeper so… can I hang out with you guys until they tire themselves out?"

Mia looked at Alex in alarm.

"He's a minor," Alex said, "but according to the laws of the province of Quebec, if he's over the age of fourteen then he can legally sign an NDA without parental consent – but we can talk about this later."

"Yeah!" Erinna agreed. "MJ, you could find passages from the Bible about the Moon and god's wrath, and maybe some whores, and the Moon turning to blood."

"I don't think there's anything in the Bible about turning the Moon to blood," Alex interjected.

"Sure there is," Mary Jane replied. "Acts 2: 19-20, 'And I will grant wonders in heaven above, and signs in the Earth beneath; blood, and fire, and vapour of smoke. The sun shall be turned into darkness, and the Moon into blood, before the great and glorious day of the Lord come. And it shall come to pass, that whoever shall call on the name of the Lord shall be saved.'"

"We definitely need you two on the team," Erinna told Mary Jane and Moshe half in jest. "In the meantime, Allen and I can get Phil to figure out what kind of industrial processes are needed to make the Moon *look* red."

"We probably shouldn't get any more people involved," Alex said. "Besides, we have teams of scientists at R&D who could help with the specifics of industrial processes and construction by-products and so on. But before we even consider going down the Operation Mindfuck route, we need to run this by John and Maggie. If they greenlight this plan –"

"To make Charles' regressive, misogynistic, anti-science batshit crazy ass look so unhinged that even his batshit crazier fan club will stop supporting the motherfucker," Allen interrupted.

"Yes," Alex agreed. "If they greenlight your *approach*, then LuNation would be able to compensate you all for you time. Mia, we can talk about this tomorrow."

"Are we all still having brunch tomorrow morning?" Othmane asked.

"We still could," Mia answered. "But I have some things to do, like figure out transportation for the next little while. I'll have to go lease a car, one that works, to get to the office on Monday."

"As I said before, I think we should all wait until Mia and I talk to the Soteros before proceeding any further," Alex insisted. "As for your transportation," she told Mia, "your compensation includes the use of a company car. We can get someone to pick you up on Monday morning at seven-thirty to beat the traffic, and you will be coming home with a loaner vehicle until you acquire your own. And another thing, we have to give this project another name than Operation Mindfuck."

"How about Operation Moonlight?" Erinna asked, to which everyone responded with a groan.

"What?" Erinna replied. "We'd all be *Moonlighting* from our day jobs at *Goddess Digest Magazine* as subcontractors..."

"No," Mia said, "but you're on the right track."

"We're not calling it Operation Disco Moon," Alex told Mia abruptly.

"Aw," Mia retorted, feigning disappointment.

"What about Moonshine?" Othmane asked.

"No thanks, I've already had a lot to drink this evening," Mia answered. "Besides, I thought you didn't drink alcohol."

"I don't," Othmane replied. "I meant 'moonshine' in the sense that it is also slang for 'bullshit'."

Mia looked at Othmane for a moment, then chuckled. "That's actually a pretty good idea," she said. "Operation Moonshine it is!"

"We'll see," Alex said finally, grabbing her briefcase and her stack of signed NDAs. She looked at Moshe, who rose to his feet and headed towards Alex to grab his own form.

"You know what?" Mia asked. "I think our secret is safe with this one. We don't need you to sign a form, do we Moshe?"

"No, aunt Mia," Moshe answered as he began to pick up the untouched trays of crackers and crudités off the coffee table. "But I want to help."

"You already have," Mia replied. "You can leave those there, I'll take care of it. But, you helped us a lot with that Bible verse. We can take it from here."

"Fine," Moshe said, placing his tray back onto the coffee table. "But I want to be kept in the loop. I want to know how it all turns out."

"That's the idea, kid," Allen told Moshe. "You'll be hearing about this all over the news!"

"*If* the Soteros are on board with this," Alex specified.

Moshe scanned the room, taking one last look at Erinna, Allen, Othmane, Mary Jane, and Alex. He turned to Mia and gave her a polite nod.

"You guys are fun!" he said in a barely audible voice as he headed upstairs, now that the occupants in the bedroom next to his had gone quiet.

Marisol Charbonneau

Chapter Fourteen

Monday morning came a little too soon for Mia. Ever the incorrigible night owl, she stayed up until well after midnight on Sunday to practice her pitch to the Soteros, with Alex's notes of course, until she passed out from exhaustion. She remembered dreaming of fantastic voyages to the Moon and of tribes of Amazon women upon it. They were clad in space suits deliberately littering the lunar surface's Earth-facing side with used menstrual products as a compelling statement of female empowerment, or something of the sort.

Then I woke up, just as things were beginning to get interesting. Dreams are funny like that.

First came the six o'clock wake-up call courtesy of Hester, followed by a quick lukewarm shower by virtue of the upstairs bathroom being shared by the younger Greenbaums this early in the morning. At seven-thirty the car came to pick up Mia for work. Mia was grateful for this, as the hearty breakfast her sister provided for her first day of work somewhat impeded the copious amounts of coffee she ingested from taking effect in a timely manner. The commute to the South Shore across the imposing and inexplicably sinuous Jacques-Cartier bridge linking the city to the farming towns-turned-suburbs, and later onto the bucolic Route 116, proved briefer by far than anything Mia expected. This was possibly because the bulk of early-morning Montreal traffic was in-bound towards the city. This, the driver told Mia, was one of the reasons why they couldn't take the quickest route to the LuNation headquarters via Victoria Bridge at the heart of Montreal's old industrial district. The narrow tracks on Victoria Bridge, the city's oldest yet paradoxically best maintained escape route off the island, only allowed for northbound traffic towards Montreal during the morning rush hour, and in the evening only to southbound vehicles.

Despite her sleep deprivation, Mia knew to heed the driver's words, as the last thing she needed right now was to find herself stuck on the way home in another magical, life-changing traffic jam courtesy of the chaotic whims of the Universe.

Though you might have the gods of Chaos to thank for this new job opportunity (if you don't fuck it all up this morning, that is). Note to self: have another cup of coffee when you get to the office, provided they allow for this during orientation. And when you get your own place, libate to the gods of Chaos as well - if everything goes according to plan. Wait, that can't be right; the gods of Chaos care nothing for the best laid plans of mortals!

"Madame Thorne?" the driver said once the car came to a full stop. They were in front of a loading bay beside a sizeable underground parking lot gradually filling up with nearly identical cars. Mia blinked groggily in the muted light, realizing that the parking lot was, in fact, fully outdoors, its shade provided by a veritable forest of solar panels held aloft by tall columns doubling as electric charging stations. In the distance, beyond the shimmering light, Mia could almost glimpse the imposing Mont-Saint-Hilaire, a colossus amidst the lesser mounts dotting the vast plain of the Saint Lawrence River Valley. Even the storied Mount Royal could not compare to the majesty that was the South Shore's holy butte.

"Madame, we are here. Maître DeBeck will be waiting for you at the main entrance. It's the big door on your right."

"Thanks," Mia told the driver as she exited the car.

"And welcome to LuNation!" the driver told her before taking off to park the car in one of the spots reserved for company vehicles.

Smart move, having a fleet of self-charging electric cars; very on-brand. And not nearly as obnoxious as Willow's half-assed carbon-footprint reduction initiative.

Mia found Alex on the other side of thick, probably bullet-proof translucent double doors in the lobby. When Alex saw Mia, she said something to the security guard, after which the doors slid open soundlessly. Mia grinned, wondering if the mechanism was fed by the solar panels in the parking lot outside.

Alex greeted Mia with a smile of her own. "Hey there," she said. "Ready to boogie?"

"No," Mia replied with utmost sincerity. "Let's do this, but first, can we make a quick stop at the cafeteria to get a cup of coffee?"

Alex let out a loud, throaty laugh, the sort of spontaneous guffaw she rarely expressed in professional settings, or at all.

And here I thought Alex stayed prim and proper even when she took a crap.

"Rough night?" Alex asked.

"No," Mia answered. "Rough morning. How early is the meeting with our Dear Leader?"

"I had it scheduled for lunch, after orientation," Alex said. "But John says he has some time before nine, so we can see him whenever you're ready."

"So orientation will be after I see the boss?"

"Pretty much."

"Depending on how well I do with the pitch?"

"Pretty much," Alex replied facetiously.

"Yeah, great, no pressure. Let's cut to the chase."

"Cafeteria is in the basement, adjacent to the gym," Alex added.

"A gym? Oooh!" Mia said. "A woman after my own heart."

"You really sound like you need caffeine," Alex said, stifling another laugh. "I hope you will find our brew... adequate."

"Now I'll be the one judging you guys. Let's boogie."

Ten minutes later, Mia followed Alex into John Sotero's office, coffee in hand, in her very own brightly coloured mug with the LuNation corporate logo. Mia asked Alex if she was allowed to keep the mug if John rejected the pitch, to which Alex answered with a shake of her head.

"If he's not on board, we'll figure out another strategy," Alex told her in the elevator. "You'll be surprised how open-minded these corporate types can be towards those who think outside the box. That's precisely why I vouched for you when John and Maggie started considering fighting back against Senator Charles by somewhat covert means.

Remember that and sip your coffee when you don't know what to say yet when he asks a question. That makes it look like you're thirsty, not unprepared. Kind of like when you sip wine after someone asks you a tough question."

Mia chuckled. "And here I thought no one noticed when I did that," she said.

"Now relax, John and Maggie are on our side. Here we are. Showtime!"

Hey wait a minute... did you just –

Alex led the way towards upper management's high-ceilinged office floor, flanked on all sides by impossibly high windows. A plump, comely, well-dressed woman sat at a broad desk before the doors leading into the Holy of Holies, smiling cordially at Alex as she walked by.

"Alex," the woman said. "John and Maggie are expecting you. And you must be Ms. Thorne. Hi, I'm Marie-Claude, Mr. Sotero's executive assistant."

"Call me Mia," Mia answered as she shook the hand that undoubtedly ran the office.

"Please, let me know if you need anything... water, tea, or coffee," Marie-Claude added.

Mia raised her mug. "I'm good, thanks," she replied with a polite nod.

Marie-Claude knocked on Sotero's door and opened it immediately, then returned to her desk, presumably to continue quietly ruling the world.

On the other side, John stood up as soon as he saw Alex and Mia, bidding them to take a seat on a couch by the low coffee table in the corner of his east-facing cavernous office. Mia blinked again in the bright morning light, barely muted by the thin photovoltaic panels between the panes of the twenty-foot-high floor-to-ceiling windows.

"Good morning ladies," John said cheerfully, taking a seat beside Maggie on the couch facing Mia and Alex. "Mia, I'm so glad you agreed to meet us before your orientation, or disorientation as our new hires call it..."

Mia took a sip of her coffee, thinking it wise not to react to John's obvious dad joke.

Do the Soteros even have children? This seems like the sort of thing I ought to know. Dang.

"Alex tells me you've been working on a strategy since you two left the party on Saturday," he added. "Let's hear it!"

Mia finally took a seat beside Alex, nodding a polite hello at Maggie, then gulped half her coffee in one swallow.

"Okay, so here's the thing," she said after a moment. "Since Senator Charles is adamant about spreading ridiculous lies about LuNation, my professional instincts tell me that we should reciprocate with a similar strategy, all the while baiting him to bury himself deeper in his web of lies by his own hand. So this is what I propose: we, and by that I mean LuNation – you – ought to fully disclose your plans to staff the lunar bases with competent, qualified women, alongside a few hand-picked high-profile men, and OWN it. Own the praise that will come when the media will inevitably tout you as a feminist hero. You're already known as a progressive on the cutting edge in your field, and you've banked on this persona you've created in the public eye for good measure. Why hold back now? So where does Charles come in, you may ask? Well, I came up with a plan that is so out of left field, that it might actually get him to back off. But... full disclosure, it's rather unorthodox."

John and Maggie looked at each other, visibly intrigued.

"We're listening," John said.

"We target Charles' informant," Mia continued, "the one who leaked Maggie's research results to his camp in the first place and have him relay information about, ahem, fictitious research findings that will stoke his holy fire. Then we have hackers plant announcements on his website about how the Lord will punish LuNation, a wicked rebellious tech-whore in the eyes of his version of the Almighty, by rendering the Moon blood-red as a harbinger of the Second Coming of Christ to rid the world of sin. We then leak an elaborate conspiracy about his own designs to spread iron oxide on the lunar surface to increase the Moon's mass until it crashes into the Earth, or something crazy like that. It doesn't matter if it's outlandish – the nuttier, the better. We then hire a discreet website optimizing firm to make sure this story goes viral, and there goes his credibility. I've got a few people, consultants really, slated to get started on this."

Mia paused, looking at John and Maggie's faces expectantly for any reaction. Unfortunately, her cheerful, sleep derived enthusiasm was met with awkward silence. After what seemed like a thousand years, John threw Alex a glance, to which she answered with a nod of approval.

"That is highly *original*," John said at last. "To be perfectly frank, I would never have come up with something like this myself."

"That is the whole point," Alex replied before Mia could provide her own ill-conceived answer. "This plan, to counter-troll your troll, is so out there that no one in a million years would ever suspect that this came from you."

John gave Mia a faint smile, which felt like a balm of relief upon her frayed nerves.

"My dear," Maggie told Mia, "that idea of yours is so crazy, it just might be brilliant. And Alex did tell us on more than one occasion how you have a most inventive mind."

Mia took a small sip of her coffee. Unclenching her jaw, she took a deep breath and said, "I do my best work thinking outside the box." She then bit her lip, though kept the mug aloft in front of her mouth so that the Soteros could not see her nervousness.

Keep it together, they are on board with this cockamamie scheme! Wait a minute – what is wrong with these two? This plan is nuttier than a squirrel's cache on the first day of winter!

"I have heard the specifics of Mia's plan in fits and starts," Alex continued. "We can only give you the broad strokes as you need to maintain plausible deniability. But the long and short of it is, since we can't have any of this be traced back to either of you personally, we will need outsiders to interface with the one we suspect to be Charles' plant. Now, we will need your authorization to approve the budget to compensate Mia's 'consultants'. I can have HR begin the vetting as soon as today."

"What kind of timeline are we looking at?" John asked.

"Provided that Charles' accomplice is who we think he is," Alex answered, "and we have security already looking into this, we could start baiting him even before we stage the press release about the lunar roster. The timing of the press release will be up to you."

John looked Mia straight in the eye. It took all of her willpower not to fall to pieces right then and there.

Note to self: libate an extra portion to thank the Gods for Alex having my back. Who's the patron god/dess of platonic long-standing friendships with your ex? It can't be Aphrodite, since we haven't done the deed in years. Is it Hera, the goddess of marriage and partnerships? Does that mean the gods mean for me to propose to Alex if we come out of this with our sanity intact?

"All right, we will give it a go," John said at last, to which Maggie gave an approving nod. "Mia, you will provide HR with a list of your 'consultants', as it were. We will compensate them for the time being from the discretionary spending account we already budgeted. Is there anything else you might need to carry this through?"

"We might need access to some of your most cutting-edge research and leak it strategically to Charles' accomplice," Mia answered, without knowing fully from whence her articulate reply came.

"And you know for certain who this person is?" Maggie asked.

"Mia's crew did some digging yesterday," Alex replied truthfully. "The man who crashed the party and accosted me on Saturday, the one who introduced himself as Brian Woodhead, is definitely not a lawyer. We have security looking into him right now, but in all likelihood he was hired to disrupt this company by pretending to recruit me and others in recent days."

"Are you certain of this?" John asked.

"Some key people at R&D have come forward to me this morning over coffee after I asked them if anyone tried to poach them recently," Alex answered. "All of them gave me a description of the culprit that matched Mr. Woodhead to a T. It's possible he might just be engaged in your garden variety brand of industrial espionage, but if that's the case, he's so inept that I wouldn't be surprised if he's working for Senator Charles."

"I have a question," Mia said. "I mean, there is something else I will need to carry this plan through. When the time will come to flesh out the details of our fictitious research results, we will need to make it look as though most of these half-truths can be backed by genuine science."

"Such as?" Maggie replied.

"First of all," Mia said, "whether there are any industrial processes that have iron oxide as a by-product, and if any of these will apply to lunar mining and whatnot."

Maggie and John looked at one another.

"Alex," Maggie said. "Tell HR to delay orientation until tomorrow. Mia needs to meet the head of R&D first."

Alex raised an eyebrow. "You mean Seth?" she asked. "I'll have Marie-Claude warn him we're coming."

Chapter Fifteen

"You *cannot* spread enough iron oxide on the surface of the Moon to increase its mass to a significant degree," Dr. Seth Hollander, the head of LuNation's Research and Development division, informed Mia over a steaming mug of mint tea in the R&D office lounge.

Alex looked at him pointedly, raising an eyebrow. Hollander relaxed and ran his hand through his mop of thick blond hair. If Mia hadn't known better, she would have thought him far too young to hold a doctorate, but then again, is seemed as though everyone looked like teenagers to Mia of late.

Granted, it could be because I am, in fact, getting older, or maybe the Willowmobile fell into a magical pothole on Autoroute 15 last Wednesday and I ended up in a parallel universe inhabited by the fae. That's probably not the case, but I ought to write a short story about this premise someday, when this is all over. I'll do that after I get my own place with a tree, then I will libate to all the gods of Earth, sea, and sky, as well as the fae, and then take a long vacation.

"Okay, let me rephrase that," Hollander continued patiently. Mia figured the lad had just remembered something Alex or Marie-Claude told him earlier about having to answer weird questions from the new hire who's working on a secret project that has something to do with public relations. "Our industrial processes on the Moon that generate iron oxide as a by-product cannot add significantly to its mass, as the materials from which the oxide would come are already there in the first place."

"So there *are* processes that create iron oxide as a by-product?" Mia asked enthusiastically.

"Yes, but –"

"So it's possible to spread vast amounts of iron oxide on the surface of the Moon to the point that it will become visible to the naked human eye from Earth?"

Hollander stared unblinkingly at Mia for a moment, his wide blue eyes betraying his befuddlement. He looked at Alex, who wordlessly prompted him to go on.

"That would take a *really* long time," he answered, "but eventually, and by that I mean after a few decades, yeah, it's possible."

Mia jotted down his words in her brand-new notebook, resisting the urge to make little happy giggly noises as she did so.

"Okay, next question, Dr. Hollander –"

"Ms. Thorne, call me Seth, please."

That's right, boy. Respect your elders.

"All right, Seth," Mia continued, "can you give me the Cliff Notes version of how one turns Moon soil into iron oxide?"

"Uh, well," Hollander stammered, "the Moon is covered with all sorts of minerals all mashed up together in layers. The elements that compose the layers on the Moon come from all sorts of things – volcanic activity, the impact of meteors striking the lunar surface, solar wind, and so on. Now, astronauts in previous Apollo lunar missions in the sixties and seventies brought back samples of minerals from the surface of the Moon, which scientists have been studying ever since. What they found out about Moon dust, especially the topmost layer called regolith, is that it's composed of a great deal of oxygen –"

"Oxygen?" Mia interrupted. "Oxygen on the Moon?"

"Yes," Hollander continued. "In the form of oxides bound together with metal alloys. Now, oxygen is very abundant in the lunar regolith, up to 45% by weight according to some metrics. And yes, there is a way to extract the oxygen through a process called molten salt electrolysis that yields powdered metals as by-products, which can also be used as building blocks in constructing habitable structures on the surface of the Moon. Iron is one such powdered metal that can result from extracting oxygen from the lunar regolith."

"This is awesome," Mia said as she frantically jotted down notes.

"But I should point out, *again*," Hollander pressed on, "that LuNation's construction teams would use these powdered metal by-products to build, well everything. Just ask Alex. We need to operate in a zero-waste capacity to comply with... what's that U.N. Space law treaty called again?"

"*The Treaty on Principles Governing the Activities of States in the Exploration and Use of Outer Space, including the Moon and Other Celestial Bodies,*" Alex answered effortlessly.

"The Outer Space Treaty," Mia added unironically, having just resisted the urge to mouth the long title as Alex recited it by rote.

"But it's the *Agreement Governing the Activities of States on the Moon and Other Celestial Bodies,* or the Moon Treaty, that bans altering the environment of extraplanetary bodies," Alex said.

"Okay, that's all fine and good, but where will the LuNation construction crews live while they're extracting oxygen and iron and things from the Moon dust?" Mia asked. "Are the spaceships that will transport them designed to turn into lunar habitats?"

Hollander looked at Alex, as if unsure whether he ought to answer.

"Ms. Thorne has the highest-level security clearance," Alex answered his tacit query. "She's asking all these questions to craft a counter-narrative to Senator Charles' public attacks against the Soteros." Turning to Mia, she added, "Just so you know, Dr. Hollander was the first among LuNation's top scientists to get contacted by Woodhead."

"Maggie gave me a quick heads up while you were on your way to the R&D wing," Hollander told Mia with a boyish smile.

Ah, so it was Maggie.

"So, just exactly how crazy yet scientifically plausible do you need your story to be?" he asked.

"Plausible enough to be provable and verifiable," Mia replied. "And batshit enough to make even the most fact-resistant religious nutjobs want to divest from associating with Senator Charles. So, as per my previous question, *where* and *how* will the first wave of lunar builders and engineers live? I presume that the ships will be large enough to accommodate heavy machinery to get everything started?"

"Yeah," Hollander said. "But we're aiming to have the crew set up residence inside lunar lava tubes to minimize exposure to ultraviolet radiation and temperature variances, not to mention space rocks crashing into the lunar surface."

"Moon caves?" Mia asked, finishing her sentence with an impish smile.

"We are fairly certain that Moon caves are without giant space worms," Hollander answered Mia's unspoken follow-up question.

"I wasn't going to imply that they were," Mia said, "but I like the way you think. Back to the matter at hand: now that we've established that it's possible to cover the lunar surface with enough powdered iron to be visible to the naked eye from Earth, would this red-brown, uh, stain, possibly reduce the effectiveness of the solar panels?"

Hollander remained silent for a moment, blinking incredulously.

"Uh, no, it would not," he answered at long last. "Not unless you covered the solar panels with powdered iron. But if you just covered the lunar surface with it, it would only slightly reduce the Moon's albedo, or the ability to reflect the sun's rays back into space, much like coal dust and debris darken glaciers and reduce their albedo here on Earth."

"So, no," Mia confirmed.

"No," Hollander repeated.

"Okay, last question: would a minimal, say, a two or three-person crew be capable of executing this sort of sabotage? To visibly cover the Moon's surface and maybe LuNation's solar panels in a relatively short period of time? Say... a few months?"

"No," Hollander replied flatly. "As I told you before, this would take several years to make a real visible impact from our vantage point here on Earth. Two people could do it, but the rest of the crew would have to be really freaking oblivious or complicit to let that happen, because even though covering large swaths of the lunar surface with iron is technically feasible, it would also be incredibly wasteful, costly, and nonsensical. Especially the latter."

"Oh, we know," Alex interjected. "But I'm pretty sure Ms. Thorne is counting on Senator Charles' supporters remaining blissfully ignorant of that fact, until we eventually point this out through official channels."

"The nuttier the story, the better it will be for all of us," Mia told Hollander. Looking up at Alex, she added, "I think I have enough to work with for the next couple of hours."

"That's good," Alex said, "because it's almost time for lunch."

"Is it really?" Mia asked, surprised that her stomach had stayed calm during her interview with the very young and shockingly patient Dr. Seth Hollander.

"Okay, can I ask you ladies a favour?" said the lad.

Mia gave Hollander a questioning look, while Alex nodded.

"Yes, you can join us for lunch," Mia answered playfully. "If that's okay with Alex and Mr. and Dr. Sotero."

"No, that's not – that's not what I meant", Hollander replied with a chuckle. "When you write this fake news counter-narrative," he continued, "can I take a look at it? Just for the sake of accuracy, or lack thereof?"

"Tell you what," Mia answered. "I really do have enough for now to get started, but when the time comes to write LuNation's official statement in response to the absolute malarkey we're about to unleash upon Senator Charles' spin doctors, I'll come see you first thing."

"Very cool," the very young man said with a puckish smirk.

Mia's stomach gave a grumble of approval.

And now for the fun part.

Marisol Charbonneau

Chapter Sixteen

At noon on Tuesday, Mia stumbled through the darkened steakhouse, looking for her co-conspirators through her oversized, expensive-looking sunglasses. The long bangs of her improbably platinum blonde wig concealed her mop of dark curls and draped her perennially youthful features. A waiter took pity on Mia and pulled open the heavy drapes of the dining room just a crack, which was enough for her to find the booth where Allen sat. Mia made a beeline towards Allen, pretending not to notice Othmane and Erinna, tablets and cell phones laid out before them, sitting at a nearby booth overlooking the table at the centre of the restaurant where Mary Jane sat alone.

Mia slid awkwardly onto the padded bench next to Allen, careful not to fall out of her disguise lest Brian Woodhead arrive early and recognize her from the previous weekend's festivities. Those took place only two blocks west of the downtown restaurant at the ground floor of Place Ville-Marie. The waiter brought Mia and Allen glasses of water and handed Mia an extra menu. As he recited the day's lunch specials, Mia spied Erinna positioning her cell phone in such a way as to fully capture the spectacle that was yet to unfold. Mia pulled out her own brand-new work cell phone and placed it where she could easily reach it should she feel the need to text instructions to Erinna and Othmane as Mary Jane demonstrated the range of her acting talents.

As soon as Operation Moonshine was approved, Alex gave HR the go-ahead to vet Allen, Erinna, Othmane, and Mary Jane as consultants working for Mia on an ad hoc basis for a confidential project. Maggie, with the help of Marie-Claude for the French version, set about to draft a simplified, media-friendly version of her research findings for the planned press release. Maggie's husband would present this to announce LuNation Mining International's plans to staff their off-world resource exploitation facilities with a largely female staff. The next phase of Operation Moonshine required LuNation's security team to confirm that Brian Woodhead was, in fact, on Senator Ethan Charles' payroll, which Allen and Othmane had verified independently on Sunday.

Armed with the certainty of Woodhead's involvement in Charles' libel campaign against the Soteros, Mia then proceeded to send Mary Jane the broad outlines of a script she would follow upon meeting with the would-be saboteur, posing as a concerned Christian member of LuNation's R&D team.

"This should be entertaining," Mia whispered to Allen once the waiter left with their orders.

"Uh-huh," Allen replied, suppressing a grin. "My bet is that Sister Christian over there will do just fine."

"I have no doubt of that," Mia said. "It's our mark that's the wild card. If he's even half as inept as he looked last Saturday, then we have our work cut out for us. Speak of the devil..."

Mia raised her phone in front of her face when she spied Woodhead entering the restaurant, his beady eyes scanning the dining hall for the elusive source willing to betray her employer to assuage her religious conscience. As Mary Jane was the only patron dining alone on this day, Woodhead walked straight to her table.

"Miss *Charest*?" he asked tentatively.

"It's pronounced 'Cariot'," Mary Jane replied.

Mia almost snorted her water, however Allen took a linen napkin and dabbed her mouth and nose before she could make a spectacle of herself.

"Miss 'Cariot'," Woodhead corrected himself, extending his hand. "Brian Woodhead, attorney at law."

Allen nudged Mia's elbow. "Dude looks like he's twelve years old," he muttered under his breath.

"Pretty much a pup in sheep's clothing," Mia agreed, giving Erinna a subtle nod as she repositioned her phone to get a better camera angle.

Woodhead took the seat facing Mary Jane. "Have you ordered yet?" he asked. "Lunch is on me, by the way."

"Thank you," Mary Jane replied politely. "No, I haven't ordered yet," she added, handing Woodhead a menu from the pile.

"Anything you recommend?" Woodhead asked.

"The prime rib is quite good here," Mary Jane answered. "That's what I'm having."

Woodhead gave Mary Jane a strange look, then nodded and opened the menu. Seconds later, he closed the menu and flagged the waiter, ordering two prime rib platters, a beer for himself, and a glass of water for his guest. Once the waiter left with their order, he turned his attention back to Mary Jane.

"So, Miss 'Cariot'," he said. "You wanted to talk about John Sotero's big announcement this afternoon, for which you have objections of a religious nature? Where would you like to begin?"

"Well that's the thing, Mr. Woodhead –"

"Call me Brian, please. Mr. Woodhead is my father."

"All right, Brian. I need to know that my employer will never find out that I spoke to you today. This can never be traced back to me."

"Of course, this conversation will be strictly confidential."

"No, you must understand, I can't lose my job. I just can't –"

"It's okay, you can tell me," Woodhead said soothingly, laying his hand atop Mary Jane's. "No one will know we spoke."

Mary Jane sighed theatrically. Taking a deep breath, she looked Woodhead in the eye and said, "This afternoon, at the press conference, John Sotero will announce that LuNation Mining International will be sending the first wave of its fleet to set up our future lunar base as early as this summer."

Woodhead nodded. "Yes, I know. I read that on their website weeks ago."

"But what you don't know is that Sotero means to staff the first wave with mostly female technicians, builders, and engineers. On purpose!"

Woodhead gave Mary Jane a quizzical look. "That's different," he replied. "But hardly objectionable from a legal and moral standpoint. Sotero is famous for being an equal-opportunity employer…"

"He'll say that he's made that decision, in consultation with LuNation's medical and scientific division, because women are more resilient against the ill effects of space travel and microgravity –"

"I read that somewhere too," Woodhead interrupted. "In the *National Geographic* or something. It's an interesting premise, but so far there's nothing really objectionable about –"

"No, you don't understand," Mary Jane insisted, her demeanor bordering on hysterical. "What Sotero is *really* doing, under the clout of extra-planetary mining, is claiming ownership of the Moon and other..."

"Celestial bodies?" Woodhead said, trying to coax Mary Jane along.

"Yeah, celestial bodies, by having the women start off-world colonies where they will reproduce asexually in outer space!"

Woodhead gave Mary Jane an incredulous stare. "Say again?"

"I know this sounds completely insane," Mary Jane continued, twisting her cloth napkin in her hands emphatically.

"I'd say," Woodhead agreed.

"But it's true! LuNation's resources have bankrolled secret labs where they perfected the process of gametogenesis, whereby one can extract DNA from the ovum of one female and combine it with that of another female, and therefore produce viable offspring. They will always be female because there are no Y chromosomes involved. It's as if they were trying to eliminate males altogether from humanity's spacefaring future! Here, I thought you might react this way and think I'm a kook, so I printed some articles from published sources talking about this from a scientific perspective!"

Mary Jane made a show of rummaging through her tote bag, then produced a stack of loosely gathered printouts and handed them to Woodhead.

Intrigued, the young man glimpsed at the printouts for a moment, then set his gaze upon Mary Jane once more.

"These articles are mostly conjectural," he said. "This procedure... gametogenesis or whatever you call it, has never been done with humans as far as I can tell. I don't specialize in medical law, but I'm pretty sure it's illegal, just as human cloning and stem cell research are still illegal."

"There is no law against either of these things in Canada," Mary Jane replied, "just as there is no law against in vitro insemination. And since LuNation's off-planet mining operations will fly under a Canadian flag, so to speak, there will be no stopping them from carrying out their plan."

"To populate the Moon and planets with Amazon women?" Woodhead asked skeptically. "Well, if it's not illegal –"

"It's not," Mary Jane conceded. "But it's just not *right*! Wouldn't you agree, as a man, that this isn't right?"

"Uh…"

"Are you a Christian?"

"Um…"

"Do you believe in God, Brian?"

"Uh… yeah, I do."

"Then as a God-fearing man, don't you think it blasphemous to go against God's plan to do away with men altogether? God created Man and Woman to multiply and be fruitful, on this Earth and in all of Creation. If He wanted the whole universe to be populated by females, would He have bothered to create Adam before Eve, even if Adam was only the first draft?"

"Oh god, you're right!" Woodhead said, looking momentarily inspired.

"Brian, we can't let them do this!" Mary Jane exclaimed with the conviction of a new convert. "This is really hard for me, as I believe in LuNation's mission to bring clean energy to the world from the Heavens above… But at what cost? You can't let Sotero bring God's wrath upon us all for disobeying His will!"

"And I won't, I promise you!" Woodhead said finally, as the waiter set the two plates of prime rib before him and Mary Jane.

"Let us say grace," Mary Jane said with unsettling calm. She bowed her head and took Woodhead's hand, then began murmuring her prayer.

Mia looked at Allen, raising her glass of water to shield her mouth from prying eyes. "I think that went well," she whispered.

Allen shook his head slightly, his eyes fixed on Woodhead, who dared not look up while Mary Jane uttered her interminable orison until she yelled out a loud "AMEN!" and began devouring her meal.

Allen grabbed his phone and texted a short message to Erinna and Othmane on the opposite side of the room. Seconds later, the pair loudly stifled their giggles, almost breaking the eerie spell Mary Jane had cast upon her newly pious dining companion. Mia took Allen's phone and read the last text he wrote, then looked at him, stone-faced, and stuffed an entire bread roll in her mouth in order not to burst into laughter. Though the screen of Allen's phone faded to black, two fateful words would remain etched upon Mia's consciousness for all time.

When this is all over, I will get my own place, with a backyard, libate to all the gods at the tree, take a long vacation, yadda, yadda, yadda, and then get a lower back tattoo proudly proclaiming these two magical words: "Namaste motherfucker".

"I'll have the cheesecake for dessert," Mia told the waiter once she swallowed her bread roll and regained the ability to speak. "With Earl Grey tea, please."

"Same for me," Allen said serenely.

"Right away," the waiter said as he left the table, probably wondering why the six patrons seated relatively close together at today's lunch service were acting so strangely on such a lovely spring day.

Chapter Seventeen

By the time Tuesday afternoon's rush hour reached its zenith, a veritable war of words was already raging on social media and other web-based purveyors of newsworthy entertainment. Literally minutes after camera crews vacated LuNation's South Shore campus at the conclusion of John Sotero's press conference, Senator Charles called for his own. The Senator was probably hoping to steal Sotero's thunder by countering his arch nemesis' magnanimous message of hope and advancement of all humankind with vague yet vitriolic accusations. Among these were claims that LuNation aimed to commit androcide by gradually eliminating males from the gene pool in lunar and other off-world human settlements in the years to come. By six o'clock that evening, television networks had joined the fray by broadcasting playback from both men's speeches on a loop, and by the time the eleven o'clock news aired, battle lines had been drawn between Senator Charles' supporters on right-wing media platforms, and Sotero's defenders on other, more reputable and scientifically literate left-leaning journalistic institutions.

By midnight, Marie-Claude welcomed Mia and Alex in John's office, where John, Maggie, and Dr. Hollander sat on the couches facing the oversize teleconference screen on the far wall.

"Good evening folks," John told the gathering, which also included the giant heads of Allen, Othmane, Erinna, and Mary Jane on-screen. "I take it we won't need to state the obvious – that this phase of Operation Moonshine worked like a charm?"

"I still can't believe that worked!" Dr. Hollander sniggered. "Did anyone else notice that the good Senator did not once go into specifics about how we allegedly intend to wipe out men from future generations? Does that seem normal to any of you in any way?"

"I believe it was Albert Einstein who said that two things in this world were infinite: the universe and human stupidity," Maggie said. "He also added that he was unsure about the universe. I'm paraphrasing, of course, but he did say that."

"I would have been shocked if *no one* had believed it, to be honest," Alex replied. "Some people will believe the craziest things if it all fits into their worldview, no matter how paranoid it may seem to the rest of us. If that weren't the case, my profession would have gone the way of the video store clerk aeons ago!"

"Be that as it may," John said cheerfully, "let me just say, well done, Mia!"

"Now, now," Mia replied humbly. "Mary Jane deserves the praise here for doing the grunt work. A round of applause for our surprisingly talented thespian!"

Allen, Othmane, and Erina cheered loudly from their end, while Mary Jane bade them to keep it down lest they wake all of Willowdale.

"We're in the basement, MJ," Allen told her. "Just take the compliment."

Another round of applause ensued, however this time Alex, Mia, Marie-Claude, and Dr. Hollander joined in.

"So, Mia," John said. "I take it that you finished the final draft of the article to upload in the good Senator's homepage?"

"Oh, yeah," Mia answered. "Seth made sure it was scientifically plausible enough to be taken as a serious threat by the authorities."

"I've got to say," Dr. Hollander interjected. "Up until tonight I really doubted whether anyone would ever be stupid enough to believe what Mia wrote about using iron oxide to turn the Moon blood-red and whatnot. But now, well, I guess anything is possible!"

"Remember what I said about Einstein, Seth," Maggie scolded him amiably.

"Yeah, I know. But damn!" Dr. Hollander added. "So we're really doing this? We're really trolling the troll? Is what we're doing even legal?"

"We'll be posting an anonymous article on Senator Charles' website," Alex answered. "Best case scenario, he'll smarten up and claim that he was hacked, deny everything, and then hopefully back off from slandering John for the foreseeable future. But knowing his M.O., he'll probably think that changing the very face of the Moon to scare sinners into repentance is pure genius, and he'll claim the idea as his own, just because. If he does that, and he probably will, then what happens next will be his own fault."

"And our hearts shall bleed purple piss for his plight," Erinna's giant head proclaimed from the teleconference screen. "So, shall we do the honours?"

Mia looked at John. "Once we open the floodgates, this can't be undone," she told him. "Anything you'd like to change in the body of the text before it gets uploaded?"

"We already dumbed it down to make it more accessible to Senator Charles' audience," Marie-Claude proudly proclaimed between sips of strong espresso. "Mia made it sound way too smart for mere mortals!"

Dr. Hollander snorted and shook his head, though he bit his lip when Maggie threw him a reproachful look.

John looked at Mia. "Proceed," he said, addressing the quartet of giant heads on the teleconference screen.

"Aye captain!" Allen replied. "And… Wait for it…"

"Done!" Othmane said finally.

And now, for the pièce de résistance – Phase Three: The Fuckening!

Marisol Charbonneau

Chapter Eighteen

After the Willowdale operatives finished hacking into Senator Charles' website to upload the dummy diatribe, Alex offered to put Mia up in her guest bedroom for the night at her place in Westmount, to which Mia readily agreed, thinking it far more considerate to her family given the lateness of the hour. Mia texted Hester to not wait up for her, then followed Alex to her car in the darkened, deserted forest of solar panels outside the LuNation campus. The drive to Alex's house was spent discussing exactly at which point Erinna's footage of the meeting between Woodhead and Mary Jane would be leaked to the press, if at all. Mia then dozed off as Alex drove across Victoria Bridge, lulled by the vibration of rubber on metal despite the bright lights of Montreal illuminating the cold spring night.

Mia was under orders to take the next morning off to recover from the previous night's off-book shenanigans, so she refrained from initiating the next phase of Operation Moonshine. LuNation still needed an official response to the good Senator's elaborately imaginative threats against John Sotero, billionaire philanthropist, and Charles' perceived ideological and romantic rival.

By daybreak on Wednesday, word of the vitriolic manifesto posted overnight on Senator Charles' website against LuNation Mining International, and other companies of its ilk, had spread across the virtual expanses of the World Wide Web faster than a zoonotic disease originating from open-air markets with questionable sanitary practices.

When Mia awoke at the crack of noon, she had yet to discover which part, exactly, of the implanted rant against the extra-planetary resource extraction industry earned the most clicks... or from whom. She found the clothes she wore the previous day laundered and neatly folded on the end table at the foot of the bed in Alex' guest bedroom. Squinting against the blinding midday sun, Mia tried to recall at what time exactly she ended up crawling into bed, clad in a too-tight shirt that obviously belonged to Alex, however she could not even remember exiting the car.

Wow. Lithe, petite Alex carried me into bed like a toddler and at some point relieved me of my clothes. Note to self: once you have your own place, yadda yadda, also take up Pilates and judo, or whatever martial arts Alex has mastered of late, and become more of a badass with the strength of ten men. Like Alex, apparently.

Donning her clothes faster than she thought possible, Mia made her way to Alex's spacious kitchen, and found her friend seated at the breakfast nook by the French doors overlooking the newly thawed garden empty of its snow dunes.

"Good afternoon," Alex said cheerfully, pouring Mia a cup of coffee.

"Hey. Did you fireman-carry me out of the car last night, strip me, and then tuck me into bed?" Mia asked casually as she took the hot mug from Alex.

"Of course not!" Alex replied, throwing her head back as she laughed heartily. "I just remembered how suggestible you get when you're half-asleep. Seriously, you're like a three-year-old when you're in an altered state. I took your clothes and handed you a nightie right after I told you to take a shower and go to bed!"

Mia blushed and bit her lip. "Uh, thanks for washing my clothes."

"No worries. Here, I made some French toast and sausages. And there's fruit salad!"

Mia took the seat facing the garden. "What's the damage report so far?" she asked as she heaped the fruit salad into her bowl.

"You'd think we threw a golden apple at a wedding we'd just crashed and weren't invited to," Alex joked.

"So, who's the fairest of them all?"

Alex raised an eyebrow. "If you mean which parts went viral the most," she answered, "then it seems as though the Religious Reich took particular exception at the suggestion that women ought to take over the space-ex industry."

"Really? Not the part where we're threatening to turn the Moon into blood? The part where we're quoting Acts 2:19-20? You know, the one that goes, 'And I shall grant great wonders in the sky above and signs on the Earth below, blood, and fire, and vapour of smoke. The sun shall be turned into darkness and the Moon into blood, before the great and glorious day of the Lord shall come.' That was the closest New Testament passage I could find that mentions the Moon turning red. Okay, Mary Jane might have helped me with this one."

"Nope," Alex answered.

"What about that passage from Jeremiah 8: 1-3, the one that Moshe mentioned the other day about what God would do to the Jews if they continued to worship the Moon? I mean, when God threatens to unearth the bones of your ancestors and lay them bare like dung upon the Earth for turning away from Him, that's a pretty damned serious threat!"

"That barely registered on the batshit sonar," Alex said.

"Okay," Mia continued. "What about the part about staging a nuclear winter by raining down space debris as a sign of God's return, as per Mark 13: 23-24? I mean, the passage goes 'But in those days, after that tribulation, the sun shall be darkened and the Moon shall not give its light, and the stars shall be fall from heaven, and the powers that are in the heavens will be shaken.' Okay, Mary Jane might have also helped me with that one."

"Not so much."

"So let me get this straight," Mia grumbled. "The pearl clutching Christo-fascists are mostly up in arms because of the part that mentions that women might end up dominating LuNation's lunar roster, even if only for purely legit – and by that I mean scientifically sound, medical and practical reasons? The part of that is *actually part of LuNation's plans* and was reported on at least six hours before our implant went live?"

"Yup."

"Wow. Seriously?"

"Yeah," Alex replied without humour. "The comments are pretty nasty, too! And graphic. And then there are those who griped about John being a person of colour in charge of providing free electricity to large swaths of the planet."

"John is Brazilian. So what?"

"Remember what sort of folks constitute Senator Charles' base," Alex answered. "Misogyny and racism are the two faces of the ultra-right wing in the United States and Canada. So much for Christian love and forbearance."

"Let me see," Mia said as she leaned over to take a glimpse at Alex's tablet.

"Better not," Alex replied, hiding the screen from view. "Our plan went exactly as expected."

"Come on, Alex. I'm a big girl!"

"Are you sure you want to see inside the cesspool, Madame Lépine?" Alex asked sharply.

Mia answered with a blank stare. "You had to go there," she said after a moment.

"Besides, isn't it a new commandment in online journalism these days to never read the comments section?" Alex said, softening her tone. "I've pretty much taken care of that for you while you slept. Here, I've got the broad lines of what you'll have to address in our press release tomorrow."

"You still want to wait a full news cycle before we react in an official manner?" Mia asked incredulously.

"Absolutely. As I said, we need to give Charles' camp a full day to categorically deny posting the implant."

"So, what's the official stance of the American Evangelical Right? And by that I don't mean the lunatic fringe. We obviously know what *they* think."

"They're all over the place," Alex replied. "But few among the sane and stalwart old guard have dared to comment on the record. I think they're waiting to see what Senator Charles will do. Until then, all bets are off."

"How long do you think that will take?"

"I'm betting we'll be hearing from his office before the six o'clock news airs on Eastern Standard Time. Here, I'm forwarding you my notes. You should receive them just about now."

"Thanks," Mia replied, digging her phone from her pocket and taking a long look at the attached text.

"You're plotting phase four of Operation Moonshine right now, aren't you?" Alex asked flatly.

"Yep."

"Slight change of plans?" she added with a grin.

"Yep."

"Whatever you're thinking, we'll have to run it by the Soteros before proceeding."

"Oh, I'm well aware," Mia replied.

"How long will it take for you to produce a presentable draft?"

"Already got the outline right here," Mia answered, tapping her temple.

"Can you write in the car on the way to work?"

Mia gave Alex a knowing smile. "I'll need to get some more caffeine in me first," she said, "but I can manage to make a lot of headway by the time we get to the office."

And this time, I won't even need to the reality-altering magic of a traffic jam to see this through!

Marisol Charbonneau

Chapter Nineteen

By Thursday morning Senator Ethan Charles, in a move that surprised absolutely no one, fully endorsed the anonymous posting uploaded to his website 36 hours prior as an on-point, biblically accurate elaboration of his personal views on the future of the space exploration industry, as well as the general role womankind ought to play in humanity's future. Also unsurprisingly, a number of prominent conservative politicians on both sides of the U.S. - Canada border wisely declined to comment on the brazen and somewhat demented rhetoric of Charles' unknown spokesperson. As a result of the ensuing confusion and uncertainty, John Sotero called for an early-morning general staff meeting to announce LuNation's official response to the recent controversy surrounding his apparent feud with Charles, and to quell worries about the company's prospects in the midst of this bizarre imbroglio.

At the LuNation South Shore campus, the atmosphere in the vast amphitheatre boardroom was downright pyretic, as all those gathered awaited with baited breath to hear Sotero's side of the disjointed and somewhat ludicrous narrative they and their fellow citizens had been told by the news media over the last few days. After most of the staff finished making their rounds at the breakfast buffet counters, John took the podium and bade Janin, his trusty I.T. technician, to open the teleconference channels and launch the presentation deck on the large screen behind him.

"Good morning, everyone!" he said in his usual warm, friendly manner.

The crowd responded in unison with a murmured greeting that came out like a vague yet powerful roar.

"Well, then," John replied affably. "I think we all know why I called you here on such short notice this beautiful morning. I guess you've all been watching the news, or reading it?"

This time some employees answered with nervous laughter while the rest gave Sotero several variations of blank, confused stares.

"Not exactly a Greek chorus, it is?' Mia whispered to Alex, who stood with Maggie by Janin's workstation to the right of the podium.

"We did a terrific job keeping all this hush-hush," Maggie replied in Alex's stead. "You can understand why most of them might feel a little stumped by all this chicanery."

"And here I come to save the day," Mia mumbled in a low voice, but loud enough for Alex to hear.

"You'll do fine," Alex told Mia. "In fifteen minutes you'll be everyone's hero. You've got this!"

"Right," Mia answered, biting her lip.

"So," John continued from the podium. "As you all might have heard by now, a certain U.S. politician is quite displeased with our company, and with me personally, for all sorts of reasons, many of which are rather esoteric? Is that the right word?"

"That guy's a nutjob!" Janin said from his workstation off-stage. Most of the gathering agreed with him enthusiastically.

"Well, I'm not a doctor of the mind," John replied, "however I can assure you all that the activities of LuNation Mining International will not, in fact, usher in the End of Days as per Scripture. It will usher in a new world of sorts, but rest assured that there is nothing we could ever do on the lunar surface that would cause the Moon to turn to blood and crash to the Earth."

This time the crowd answered with good-natured laughter, until someone yelled out:

"What about our stock prices?"

Mia craned her neck to see who had killed the mood, figuring the question came from the accounting gaggle still crowding the buffet table at the back.

"Interesting you should ask," John answered. "Our stocks have not taken a significant hit so far, only a slight dip, and we intend to keep it from dropping further than that. That is why I wanted all of you here to listen to our response to the preposterous tirade on Senator Charles' website, including those of you working from home and in our satellite offices. And for our colleagues on the other side of the globe where it is still the middle of the night, this meeting will be recorded and uploaded on the company Intranet within the hour. So, without further ado, let me introduce our new Chief Communications Officer, whom some of you have already met this past week. We hired her on a permanent basis to help us mitigate such assaults on our reputation, and to serve as liaison to help educate the public on what it is we actually do on Earth and plan to do in outer space. So please give a warm welcome to our new colleague, Ms. Neomia Thorne... Mia?"

Preceded by hesitant and under-caffeinated applause from the gathering, Mia took John's place at the podium.

"Good morning everyone," she said, placing her cue cards on the podium's surface. "I guess I'll get right to the point: I've been tasked with drafting an official response to the events that have come to light in the past few days, and you will be the first to hear it before it goes live on our corporate news feed, so here it goes:

"Yesterday, an anonymous article appeared on U.S. Senator Ethan Charles' official web page, which made bold, apocalyptic allegations as to the true intent of LuNation Mining International, and of the company's founder and CEO, Giovanni Sotero, with regards to our plans to set up solar panels on the Moon to power our lunar resource extraction bases. According to this anonymous jeremiad, Mr. Sotero, using LuNation Mining International as an elaborate front for his blasphemous ends, means to put an end to our civilization by colonizing the Moon with women engineers whose ultimate goal is to destroy the world economy by harnessing the energy of our sun and beaming the solar power back to Earth and distribute it to all nations of the world free of charge. This, the anonymous poster charges, will cause massive social unrest across the globe, and especially in the United States of America, as it will destroy the coal and oil industries in that nation, and teach women that they can take over the extra-planetary resource extraction industry without divinely mandated male guidance. We will address the latter point in a bit, but first we need to confront the allegations that LuNation Mining International's activities mean to intentionally wreak havoc upon the world economy.

"While it is true and accurate that LuNation Mining International plans to install a vast array of solar panels on the Moon in part to power our extra-planetary resource extraction activities, it is absolutely false that these

activities aim to irreparably harm the world economy, or the U.S. economy specifically. The fact of the matter is that the energy generated by LuNation's off-world solar panels will far exceed the needs of our on-site lunar installations. In light of our calculations, our company, with the collaboration of a number of intergovernmental organizations on all five continents, many of which include the United States as a member state, has agreed to beam most of the energy generated by our solar panels to power receptor plants located in several countries around the Earth's equator. This process aims to greatly improve living conditions in all nations of the world, especially developing nations that will have improved access to free and clean energy with all its associated benefits. This will also provide a viable and sustainable alternative to the use of energy generated by the fossil fuel industry, which we know to be a crucial step in halting the devastating effects of climate change and ensuring a future for our children, and for all life on Earth.

"Today Senator Charles has sanctioned the views that were described in the anonymous post as reflective of his own. Taking into account that Senator Charles has for years used his family's fortune in the oil industry to finance his political career and rise to prominence, the reasons behind his endorsement of this anonymous post become self-evident. Senator Charles has a well-documented record of opposing the implementation of clean energy technologies, and of using his power and influence to block legislative efforts to curb carbon emissions in his home state and his country, ignoring decades of warnings from the scientific community and from grassroots environmental protection organizations from around the globe. Senator Charles has often publicly repudiated studies discussing the impending threat of climate change, not only for his own behalf, but also for many of his constituents who depend on the extraction of depleting oil reserves in the United States and other nations to maintain their wealth, their status, and their privileged way of life.

"In recent years, Senator Charles began framing in religious terms his objections to the U.S. economy divesting from the extraction and use of fossil fuels on a mass scale. In doing so, he has convinced his pious followers and constituents that his position is in accordance with the will of Providence with regards to humankind claiming dominion upon the bounty of the Earth and all associated resources for the benefit of one species and to the detriment of all others on this planet we call home.

"*Unlike Senator Charles, LuNation Mining International does not comment upon matters of faith as to the rightness of our actions before the will of the Almighty. We do, however, proclaim that our actions will prove a boon to humankind, in this world, for generations to come. We will never apologize for contributing, in the most concrete way available to us at our level of technological advancement, to help developing nations take control over matters of energy redistribution that others have taken for granted over the course of generations because of the accidental privilege of their births. We will also never apologize to the fossil fuel industry oligarchs for challenging their supremacy by offering to the nations of the world a viable, clean and sustainable energy alternative by channelling the power of our sun for the benefit of billions. We will never apologize for offering to the developing nations of the world a chance to meet the international community on an even keel and for giving them what they are owed, for the wealthy nations could never have achieved their current state of political ascendancy and material comfort without exploiting colonized territories for centuries.*

"*Finally, we at LuNation Mining International will never apologize for treating women and men as equals in our hiring practices or for basing our off-world staffing decisions on research conducted by our esteemed colleagues in the scientific community. If Senator Charles takes exception to the fact that women are more resistant than men to space sickness and other ill effects of prolonged exposure to microgravity, then perhaps he ought to take his complaints to his Creator instead of sullying the name of our founder and CEO. Giovanni Sotero is a well-liked public figure who has throughout his career made genuine efforts to improve the lot of his fellow human beings, no matter their gender, sexual preference, or ethnicity. Senator Charles, on his part, has not only turned a blind eye, but actively derailed efforts to bring to justice a number of workers in his own fossil fuel extraction conglomerate, who have committed great acts of violence against Indigenous women and girls in the oil fields and 'man camps' of the North American plains. We at LuNation Mining International abhor and repudiate such blatant miscarriages of justice in the name of egoistical capitalism that would plunder the Earth for profit until no resource is left unexploited.*

"*On a final note, let us address the assertion, which Senator Charles endorses, that LuNation Mining International's leadership means to spit in the face of the divinely mandated patriarchal status quo by sending women on extra-planetary mission to colonize outer space without adult male supervision – or even the seed of their loins. By far, this is the most outrageous accusation levelled against our company, yet we have no choice but get at the root of this ridiculous notion. In the last 24 hours our security services have uncovered an elaborate prank instigated by a little-known anarchist group who call themselves 'Erisian Fields'. This group has a confirmed foothold in the city of Montreal, yet so far we know very little else about them. One of their operatives, who posed as an employee of LuNation Mining International, baited one of Senator Charles' staff in the city this week. You will find below a link to video footage of a meeting between a woman identified as Judy S. Charest – which we are told was a pseudonym... baiting a certain Mr. Brian Woodhead, who claims to be an attorney in the service of Senator Ethan Charles, into believing that Mr. Sotero's intent for his company's activities are far less orthodox than the liberal press would have us believe."*

Mia grabbed hold of the projection screen remote control and mumbled in her microphone, "Bear with me folks, this is my first week."

As the crowd laughed from the welcome levity, Janin stood up to help Mia find the button to access the video file of the footage. "There we are!" Mia spoke in the microphone. "Janin, take it away!"

The young I.T. technician pointed the remote at the screen, after which a pop-up window appeared, revealing a still shot of a woman with a heavily pixelated face and a young man seated at a table in a well-known downtown Montreal steakhouse. Janin activated the video and stepped aside from the front of the projector screen, prompting Mia to do the same.

Woodhead's encounter with Mary Jane played out in its entirety, its magnificent awkwardness displayed for all to see.

"All that is left to say," Mia declared once the video ran its length time, "is that the woman featured in this video is not, in fact, an employee of LuNation Mining International. What you all saw constitutes an elaborate hoax, ladies and gentlemen, of which LuNation Mining International took no part. This video, as well as the speech you just heard, will be made available to the public at large on our corporate website as of noon today. I will also be giving a press conference at that time in the atrium, so I will ask all of you to remain on the mezzanine upstairs to show your support for our company, and to allow journalists access to our facilities. I also ask that you share the link to this press release your personal and professional social media websites in the following hours. If there are any other questions, I will be more than glad to answer them directly once they are sent to my direct email, which is now listed in the employee directory. Thank you for your time, ladies and gentlemen, and other! You can also find me at my office on the third floor. Thank you."

The crowd applauded as Mia exited the podium and joined John, Maggie, and Alex off-stage by Janin's workstation.

"I think that went well," Alex told Mia.

"Not bad for a dry-run," Mia replied. "Now I'll have to do this again, in front of cameras."

"You knocked it out of the park," Maggie said. "Isn't that right, John?"

Mia, Alex, Maggie, and Janin all turned their gaze toward John, who stared back at them all with an amused grin.

"Judy S. *Cariot*?" he asked.

"Judas Iscariot, who betrayed Christ for thirty pieces of silver," Mia replied. "Mary Jane has a twisted, yet very biblically sophisticated sense of humour. She used to be almost a nun, you know, but I think she missed her true calling as a character actress. Anyway, once this all blows over, I'll introduce you all, but just not in a steakhouse."

Marisol Charbonneau

Chapter Twenty

To the surprise of absolutely no one on either side of the Canada-United States border, Senator Charles responded to LuNation Mining International's Thursday press release by targeting his foe's eloquent, charismatic, and innocuous spokeswoman. First came the predictable smears against Mia's scant communications and marketing experience as a former junior writer for a "hippie feminazi publication" according to some right-wing wags volunteering as Charles' mouthpieces. Then Mia's supposed dilettantism came to light due to her inconsistent employment history while attending graduate school at the crone-like age of thirty-five. Though Mia's professional credentials were fair game as a matter of public record, Charles' camp holding her responsible for the difficulties navigating the labour market in Canada's National Capital Region while juggling schoolwork looked like a desperate grab of low-hanging fruit to even the orneriest conservative pundits in the Bible Belt. By Friday mid-afternoon, just as the North American viewership threatened to lose interest in Charles' inane vendetta against a Solarpunk titan of industry and his messenger, the Senator held an impromptu press conference of his own outside his office in Washington, D.C. There, a faction of his supporters escalated the wrangle to an alarming degree by chanting "Burn the Witch!" whenever Charles mentioned Mia by name.

Though separated from her southern neighbours' asininity by an international border and buffered by the relative sanity of a pluralistic metropolis in a post-religious province, Mia took the threat seriously enough to abscond from her sister's home with only her backpack and the clothes on her back. Shortly before sundown on Friday evening, she had relocated to the relative safety and seclusion of Alex's Westmount abode, under a 24-hour police protection order until further notice. For the first time since her divorce, Mia consumed a veritable elephant dose of sedatives to sleep that night. Unbeknownst to Mia, Alex stayed up until well past midnight to hide the bottles of hard liquor lest Mia sleepwalk to the living room bar and serve herself a hefty drink to soothe her frayed nerves, accidentally poisoning herself to death before the crazies got the chance to do her in.

Marisol Charbonneau

On Saturday morning, Mia awoke in a daze of incredulity, which a very sleep-deprived Alex tried to counter by brewing enough coffee to power a literary convention for a full three-day weekend. Their combined stupor proved blessedly brief, for shortly after breakfast a vehicle belonging to Willow's motley fleet appeared on Alex's street, its way barred by the police cruiser blocking the narrow driveway. Clad in her Armani bathrobe, Alex met her visitors on the curb, then assured the young officer assigned to protect her and Mia that Dr. Phil Raven, Mama Willow Moon Raven Rhiannon the Wise, and their young daughter Katie did not present a threat to herself or her houseguest.

Alex bade her visitors to follow her to the kitchen, where they found Mia seated at the table by the French doors, clutching her oversize coffee mug as if holding on to dear life.

"So, I'll leave you guys to it," Alex said. "If you need anything, I'll just be right here, loading the dishwasher."

Mia looked up at the newcomers incredulously.

"There were three Ravens," Katie said for the sake of levity.

"Sat on a tree?" Mia replied, to which Phil nodded emphatically, while Willow remained impassive.

"So I guess you all heard about-" Mia continued, gesturing at everything around her.

"Yeah," Phil said. "It's all so... special, but now our conversation from last week is starting to make a lot more sense. But still. Wow."

"Yeah, I didn't imagine *this* would happen, not in a million years," Mia replied. To Willow, she said, "I'm really sorry I got the Magazine dragged into this..."

"You didn't, Mia," Willow said. "Those fundie douche nozzles dragged us into it, and *it's on!*"

Mia raised an eyebrow. Phil and Katie looked at her with their heads slightly tilted to the side, while Alex poked her head above the counter, momentarily distracted from her housekeeping by Willow's outburst.

So much for love and light, thoughts and prayers, and tolerating unconditionally those who do not think like us...

"We had a little talk," Phil said diplomatically, "Willow and Allen and I –"

"We want you to know that we're behind you a hundred percent," Willow interrupted heatedly. "Right now, we've got the entire staff at *Goddess Digest Magazine* issuing a call to arms to the entire Pagan community from here to Toronto to Halifax, and even Vermont and all across New England! *This. Will. Not. Stand!* An attack on one of us is an attack on us all!"

"Um, okay," Mia stammered, somewhat confused by Willow's unexpected and uncharacteristic channelling of her inner warrior goddess. "So, what are..."

"We're doing a *huge* warding spell!" Katie blurted out with glee. "In the woods! Everyone will be there! It's going to be EPIC!!!"

Phil nodded.

"I have so many questions," Mia whispered absentmindedly.

As Willow opened her mouth to retort, the doorbell rang, prompting Alex to jog to the front door. Glancing at the hallway, Mia noticed that Alex somehow managed to get fully dressed in the five-odd minutes between Phil, Willow, and Katie's arrival and the loading of the dishwasher. Given the chain of events that unfolded in the last few days alone, Mia found herself on the verge of determining that Alex was, perhaps, one of the fae.

That would explain so many things...

"God won't mind my driving all this way from the other side of town on the Sabbath," Mia heard a familiar voice kvetch from the end of the hallway. "My little sister needs me!"

"Tia?" Mia said, as Hester made her way towards the kitchen, with Moshe at her heels.

Mia spotted some articles of her own clothing protruding from the top of one of the bags Hester carried, while Moshe held a rather large box filled to the brim with food containers, which Alex took from the lad and placed on the kitchen counter. Hester gave Mia a warm smile and motioned to embrace her, however her face blanched and she froze in her tracks as soon as she recognized at least two of the other three visitors in Alex's kitchen.

Alex bit her lip, realizing her *faux pas* of not warning Hester that her ex-husband, his wife, and their child were also in her home.

"Oh... darn," Alex exclaimed when the awkward silence became too much for her fatigued nerves to bear.

"Katie," Mia said to cut the tension. "This is my sister, Hester, formerly Hestia, and my nephew, Moshe. Hester, Moshe, this is Katie, child spy prodigy *extraordinaire*."

"Hello Katie," Hester said, giving the girl a polite nod.

"Hey," Moshe said.

"Shalom," Katie replied artlessly.

"Katie, why don't you help Moshe take the bags to my room?" Mia suggested. "If you don't mind? It's upstairs, all the way down the hall."

"Sure," Katie acquiesced, as Moshe began unburdening Hester and handed Katie the lightest bag.

"Cute kid," Hester said casually once Moshe and Katie left the room. "How old is she?"

"Almost fifteen," Mia answered before Willow could say a word.

"Fourteen and a half," Willow retorted. "Before you start counting."

"Where do you get off –" Hester said, before Phil made a hand gesture to draw attention to himself.

"Look," he interjected. "I think we can put aside our... differences for the moment, and all agree that we're here to support Mia."

"Right," Hester agreed. "Well, Mia, Moshe, and I brought you your things. It goes without saying that you are welcome to return to our home whenever you feel safe to do so. Ira and the children send you their best and want you to know that as long as there are Greenbaums in Montreal, you will never come to harm."

Mia bit her lip. She tried to say something, but remained visibly shaken from all that transpired since the last Full Moon.

"Willow and her crew will be staging a massive ritual in the woods up north tomorrow," Alex said to change the subject. "What did Katie call it? A warding?"

"To protect one from harm," Hester answered. "I've heard of such things done before. Like when the Witches in the New Forest did a ritual involving all the covens in England to ward Hitler's army off their shores during the Second World War."

"We'll be doing that, though not exactly," Willow said.

"Well, no, pretty much exactly from what I understand," Mia replied. "It might be too early in the season for a *skyclad* ritual, though on the plus side there aren't many mosquitos out and about yet."

"Skyclad?" Alex asked.

"In the nude," Phil answered casually. "Clad with the sky. The theory is that clothing dampens the flow of energy, so that's why the Witches do their magical workings naked."

"Awesome," Alex said tonelessly.

"It won't be skyclad," Willow said. "There will be news coverage of the event, so that we can send a message to fundie fuck-nuts everywhere that we are a force to be reckoned with!"

"How can I help?" Hester asked, eliciting a surprised look from Willow, Phil and Mia, as well as a questioning stare from Alex.

"What?" Hester continued. "I studied theatrical production and stagecraft back in University!"

"Right," Alex replied. "Sorry, I completely forgot about that."

"It's all right," Hester said. "I may not have worked professionally in my field, however I got to do plenty of stage direction raising almost an entire hockey team over the last fifteen years."

"I'll bet," Alex chuckled.

"That would be... wonderful," Willow said, surprising everyone. "Thank you, Tia."

"It's Hester," Mia and Hester replied in unison.

"Right," Willow replied. "Sorry, still getting used to it –"

"Yeah, adding the passage about God punishing Israel for playing the whore and courting foreign gods was totally my idea," Moshe told Katie as the two returned to the kitchen, their faces aglow with wide, goofy grins.

Phil threw Mia a knowing glance as Hester and Willow raised their eyebrows in perfect synch.

Alex bit her lip.

Mia sighed at her sister and her former boss' combined naiveté.

What, you didn't know? This outcome was inevitable from the moment the traffic came to a complete halt on Autoroute 15 two weeks ago due to an overturned car, Gods of Chaos be praised!

Chapter Twenty-One

Sunday proved unseasonably warm in the hilly country north of Montreal, where in the first weeks of May the lingering bite of winter sometimes threatens to cover the forests with a dusting of snow late at night. However, on this evening the warm spring breezes persisted until well after sunset and the rising of the waning gibbous moon, a most auspicious time to banish foes or to perform a warding ritual against a nuisance. As the stars began to appear in the northern skies above the treetops surrounding the manor belonging to Lady Pythia, Internet sensation and Oracle to Quebec's entertainment media elite, an eclectic crowd began to gather in clusters in Pythia's vast backyard. A handful of torches were lit around the perimeter of the clearing for the benefit of the news camera crews come to record the proceedings, as well as Allen and Othmane who were tasked with broadcasting the festivities for Mia via videoconference.

From the safety of Alex's living room, Mia spied Hester directing the new arrivals to their places around the perimeter of an unseen circle. Hester was seemingly unfazed by their brightly coloured vestments and phantasmagorical costumes, which by some small miracle remained uncannily conspicuous even in the growing darkness of the boreal night. Mia also saw her reminding the reporters congregating on the site that they could not begin filming until all participants who wished to remain anonymous put on their masks. Beside her stood Mary Jane, to whom Hester redirected the participants new to the concept of a protest-cum-theatrical magical working. In turn, Mary Jane sent the novices to learn the ritual outline from Luna Rowan Moonbeam, copywriter for *Goddess Digest Magazine* and mediocre cook, and the chants from Katie, skilled in song thanks to her liberal-arts-focused high school curriculum. Neither Hester nor Mary Jane batted an eye when Othmane remarked that a few members of the Montreal Satanist chapter roamed the woods behind the treeline. As it turned out, the eco-friendly, socially conscious, activist worshippers of the Dark Lord heard about Willow's get-together through the occult grapevine and volunteered to provide security against any unwelcome interloper intent on mischief.

"They're all wearing black robes!" Mia heard Othmane say off-camera.

"Well, duh!" Allen retorted. "You wouldn't wear a bright pink unicorn costume either if you planned on hiding in the woods after dark!"

"No," Othmane acquiesced. "I suppose not. Those wearing the neon pink unicorn outfits are right there, front and centre, distracting people away from the woods. I've seen five of them so far. Are you seeing this, Mia?"

"Yes," Mia said. "And I'll bet you a cheeseburger that Dennis put his group up to this."

"That's the Discordian who preaches from his van in the parking lot of the giant orange thingy by Autoroute 15 on Decarie?" Alex asked as she filled her glass and Mia's with a copious amount of red wine.

"The very same," Mia replied. "Tell me," Mia asked from the other side of the screen. "Who else is there with you?"

"Well," Allen answered, "pretty much everyone even remotely involved in the Pagan or magical communities this side of the Great Lakes."

"Our call to arms was very thorough," Othmane added.

"How thorough, you may ask?" Allen continued. "Look over there by the North Quarter, you've got a substantial number of people from two coven trads from the Pagan communities in the Laurentians. They're likely the only public Pagan groups from here to the Arctic Circle and they're surrounded on either side by a bunch of covens from Montreal and the South Shore. At the East Quarter we have three... *three* regional Druid groves, one of which drove in from Moncton just this afternoon. At the South Quarter we have assorted eclectics, basically the least experienced of the bunch, which is why MJ keeps sending them towards Luna and Katie. At the West we have many Elders from Indigenous communities and their entourage and other locals. And here is our Mistress of ceremony coming out of Pythia's house, all dolled up in her ritual robes. Yo, Willow! Come say hello to Mia –"

"I thought the Indigenous spirituality revival and Neo-Paganism were completely different things," Alex told Mia while Allen was distracted by his boss' arrival.

"They are, sort of," Mia explained. "But there's a lot of overlap, philosophically speaking."

"And a lot of the Indigenous communities are mad as hell at Senator Charles and his Big Oil operations in the Western provinces," Allen said. "So there's that."

"A lot of people here are not necessarily involved in the Craft," Willow said, having clearly overheard the last part of the on-screen conversation from her end. "But that's fine with us, as we're all here for the same reason: to protest the egregious position taken by Senator Charles and all his racist, misogynistic, Earth-poisoning supporters motivated only by evil and greed."

Mia squinted at the large screen on Alex's living room wall, then realized that Willow was not speaking to her directly, but rather to a small army of reporters barely illuminated by torchlight.

"Also," Willow continued, her back turned away from Allen's camera, "many people are here to show support for a member of the *Goddess Digest Magazine* family, Mia Thorne, who has unfairly become the target of death threats from the right-wing lunatic fringe in both Canada and the U.S. To those who would do her harm, the people here gathered in this place have a message. There are more of us forward-looking people of all faiths, races, etc. who want a just and equitable world for our children and our children's children, and we will *absolutely* mobilize to see this happen. We will not sit idle while you destroy the Earth for profit any longer, now that a true alternative exists. We will boycott you and your cronies until you crawl back into the hole from whence you came, and if you so much as threaten one of us as we do our holy work, then you will have to answer to *all of us*!"

"All of us!" the crowd cheered, as the still-forming circle of celebrants gathered into formation. An eerie silence fell over the crowd as the people reached out to hold hands.

"Are they casting the Circle?" Alex asked.

"Looks like it, or a reasonable facsimile thereof," Mia replied as she drank deeply of her wine. "I don't know if they'll call the Quarters and invoke the Elements in the traditional way. I guess the specifics don't really matter, since this is theatre."

"Whatever they do, it's probably already worked," Alex said, pointing to her cell phone lighting up with several messages all at once.

"Should I ask?" Mia inquired.

"Looks like you and John will be doing the media circus rounds over the next few days," Alex answered. "He's already got several interview requests from both sides of the border since Friday, but that number tripled in the last five minutes alone."

"Hold on," Mia said haltingly. "This is being broadcast *live*? Not a recorded puff piece for a slow news day?"

"No," Allen retorted from behind the camera. "We're live, and the whole world is watching," he added while panning the camera towards the shield-wall of camera crews behind the row of reporters.

"That's... a lot of people," Mia said, genuinely amazed by the sheer numbers of human beings gathered at the warding ritual held in her honour.

"So far it's going without a hitch," Allen replied. "Hey Othmane, remind Mary Jane to pitch to Willow a story about the Satanists, who are probably to thank for this going so well."

"Do you think the Discordians and the Satanists are working as a team?" Othmane asked.

"That's an awful lot of organizing for a bunch of anarchists," Allen answered. "The Satanists organize. The Discordians wing it."

"The two are not mutually exclusive!" Alex remarked before taking a dainty sip of her wine. Looking at Mia, she asked, "are you okay?"

"Yeah," Mia replied. "I kind of wish I were there, but the cops strongly advised against it. You know."

"Yeah, I know," Alex agreed. "Hopefully, this will all be over soon."

"I hope so," Mia said wistfully. "After John and I run the media gauntlet."

"Don't worry, I'll be handling the Press," Alex replied.

Mia raised an eyebrow.

"What?" Alex asked. "I meant the legal stuff. *Of course* you'll be the one in front of the camera. Like John, you've also become the official face of LuNation Mining International."

"That was the job I agreed to," Mia conceded. "To expose that Senator Charles bastard by any covert and unconventional means necessary."

"And you succeeded," Alex said.

"You mean, this?" Mia asked, gesturing at the colourful spectacle on the living room screen.

"I mean this, exactly," Alex replied. "If staging a Witches' Sabbat in the woods to stick it to the man isn't considered unconventional, I don't know what is."

"True, although putting that *papier maché* effigy of Charles in the centre of the circle is a bridge too far, considering some of his supporters threatened to do the same to me, only literally."

"I don't think that's an effigy for burning," Alex said. "That's a piñata."

Mia spat out her wine on Alex's polished marble coffee table.

Alex laughed. "Okay, I'm *so* glad right now that I had the white carpets removed before moving in," she said, catching her breath. "But still, even if I hadn't, that would have been worth the cost of dry-cleaning just to see the look on your face right now! Hold on, let me take a picture..."

"Oh boo!" Mia replied once she regained her dignity. "The Discordians strike again."

"Who said it was the Discordians' idea?" Alex joked. "I think you have Discordians on the brain. You're not thinking of joining them, are you?"

Mia raised an eyebrow. "Do I look like I have *any patience left*, what with being threatened with the White American Evangelical Inquisition only a week after running away and leaving the circus after Willow got on my last nerve?"

"From the looks of it," Alex replied, "these Pagans are anything but a monolithic block."

"Okay," Mia retorted. "Granted, maybe I was, at times, a bit harsh in my personal judgment of Pagans before this whole thing launched into the stratosphere. But I've got to hand it to Willow, she did bring people together!"

"I'm pretty sure you had something to do with it," Alex said.

"I didn't bring them together with my prose," Mia replied. "I just gave them a common enemy!"

"That's usually how alliances work," Alex quipped. "Here, have some more wine."

As Alex poured the remainder of the wine in Mia's cup, Allen stepped in front of his camera and said, "Ladies, there is someone I'd like you to meet. Hathor? Come over here, I'll introduce you. Here, hold on..."

Allen turned the camera to the left as an attractive, thirty-something woman came into view. Mia thought her costume looked familiar, though in her slightly tipsy state she could not quite recall exactly why.

"It's okay," Allen told the woman, who looked somewhat embarrassed for reasons Mia suspected would soon become clear. "Hathor, this is Mia, the one who was on TV, and that is her friend Alex who works with her. Alex is the lawyer at LuNation. You can tell them what you just told me."

"I'd rather not do this on camera," the woman mumbled almost inaudibly, her eyes downcast. "Can I call you instead? Maybe from inside the house where it's private?"

"Sure, Hathor," Mia said.

"And I would like to talk to Alex, the lawyer, if you don't mind," Hathor said.

"Uh, sure," Alex replied. "Call my home office line, I'm messaging it to Allen via the video conference chat right now. Call when you're ready, we're not going anywhere."

The woman, Hathor, nodded gratefully and made a beeline towards Pythia's house, then disappeared from the screen.

"What's going on, Allen?" Mia asked as Alex power-walked to her study, closing the door behind her.

"Let Alex handle it," Allen answered, "but trust me, it's a doozie."

Before Mia could reply, Alex's phone rang. Alex picked up the receiver almost immediately, however Mia could not overhear Alex's end of the conversation from the living room couch. Left to her own devices, Mia turned her attention back to the screen and smiled at a familiar face staring back at her with a beatific, albeit slightly goofy grin.

"Hey Mia," Othmane said. "Where did Alex go?"

"She's on the phone," Mia replied casually. "So, was this your first public Pagan ritual?"

"Yes," Othmane answered giddily, as Alex strode out of her study hastily, her wireless phone in hand.

"And you have proof of this?" Alex spoke into the phone, nodding emphatically as she looked at Mia. "No, you won't get into trouble," she continued. "And if you weren't a minor when it happened, then your congregation won't be liable either... Can you meet us at LuNation's offices tomorrow morning? Do you know where? Yes? Okay, nine o'clock? Okay. A quick heads up, there will be a police presence, but that's for Ms. Thorne. Don't be alarmed, we had to beef up security since Friday because... Yeah. You will be perfectly safe. Thanks. We'll see you tomorrow."

"Let me guess," Mia said, suddenly remembering where she had seen Hathor's elaborately ornate costume during her short tenure as a journalist for a widely read Pagan publication. "Someone has a sex tape of you-know-who involving the space orgy people?"

Alex nodded. "And if this pans out the way I think it will," she told Mia, "then don't ever let me hear you speak ill of magic and Witchcraft ever again!"

Mia bit her lip.

I never said magic didn't work.

Chapter Twenty-Two

The following Friday, on the night of the new moon, Mia sat in the make-up room of yet another long-running, highly rated, late-night cable television programme, waiting for the production assistant to instruct her when to take centre stage before a live studio audience. Mia knew the show's host, Will Baher, by his reputation as a controversial comedian whose main act consisted of editorializing current events satirically, yet not without showing empathy for his put-upon guests from either side of the political divide. This made some of his audience consider him a more trustworthy news source than most broadcast media, and his rants often went viral in ways that predictably went awry for all the right reasons. Unlike many reporters and talk show hosts who had interviewed Mia or John Sotero over the last week, the famously humanistic and free-thinking Baher seemed the most likely television personality to paint Mia and her employer as plucky heroes against a powerful, albeit obtuse and fanatical goliath. At least that was Mia told herself before the show's producers told her that they had also invited Betty Vaughan, Senator Charles' spokesperson and rumoured mistress, to join tonight's panel.

At least they had the decency to have Vaughan join via satellite for tonight's episode, Mia thought as she dabbed the excess lipstick off her lips on a thin ply of tissue paper.

On second thought, decency and consideration probably had very little to do with it. After all, Charles' mouthpiece was currently in Washington, D.C., whereas *In Synch With Will Baher* was filmed in New York City, where many of Charles' staff and supporters seldom dared to tread.

"We're ready for you, Ms. Thorne," the barely shaving junior production assistant told Mia at last.

"Right," Mia said as her fingers danced on the screen of her cutting-edge smartphone. "Done."

Knock'em dead, said one reply.

The phone subsequently lit up with various iterations of the same message from Alex, John and Maggie, Allen, Phil, and even the young Dr. Seth Hollander, who took great delight in his role as John and Mia's scientific consultant during their week-long media gauntlet. Mia followed the fledgling production assistant with the oversize headphones and clipboard down a maze of stage props and equipment towards Baher's trademark large pentagonal glass desk, where she sat in the seat opposite her host's. The houselights above the desk dimmed, relegating Mia to the shadows in anticipation for Baher's opening monologue, consisting of the first sequence of the programme.

As Baher walked onto the stage to thunderous applause from the studio audience, Mia took long, calming breaths, barely paying any attention to her host's clever quips about the latest gaffes of the American and international political intelligentsia.

Just remember what you've done at every show you've been on this week. As long as you insist upon Charles' culpability in escalating the vendetta he initiated against John months before you even started working for him, you'll remain in control of the narrative.

"And now here is my first guest, who you'll recognize as one of the main characters of the latest reality show, 'Senator Ethan Charles' Tin Foil Hat Brigade versus Brazilian Tony Stark'," Baher said to the camera before pausing for the audience's laughter. "Ladies and gentlemen, Mia Thorne."

Mia opened her eyes and affected a demure smile as Camera Three focused on her, while Baher made his way to his desk and greeted his guest.

"Welcome Mia," Baher said, to which Mia answered with a practiced nod.

"Before we add my next guest to the panel," Baher continued, "I would just like to ask, because I know you are a real journalist, and that you did your undergraduate degree in... anthropology? Is that right?"

"That is correct, cultural anthropology," Mia answered.

"So in your years studying cultural anthropology and journalism, did you ever think you'd find yourself at the centre of a media circus pitting one of the world's foremost space mining promoters and philanthropists, with the… let's just call it what it is – America's answer to the Spanish Inquisition?"

"Well, Will, I don't think anyone really expects the Spanish Inquisition, American or otherwise, so no," Mia replied to the sound of uproarious laughter from the crowd.

"Okay, I walked right onto that one," Will chuckled. "But seriously. How crazy have the last two weeks been for you? I mean, you took a job at LuNation Mining International just before the infamous steakhouse video went viral – you all know which one, with that lady 'Judas Iscariot' character playing a genius prank on Senator Ethan Charles' own novice attorney. Did you ever guess, in a million years, that things would blow up on the international stage as they did?"

"Like I said," Mia answered. "No one could ever predict the sheer scale of escalation for an already extremely complicated situation."

"You're referring to Senator Charles' prior objections to John Sotero, your boss, and his work in space mining and such," Baher inquired.

"I'm referring to Senator Charles' objections to Mr. Sotero's plan to provide clean energy to the whole world as a by-product of our off-world mining operations," Mia corrected him. "Especially to developing nations, who stand to gain the most from obtaining unfettered access to levels of energy on par with those of industrialized nations."

"So it wasn't about religion," Baher said.

"No, we don't think so," Mia retorted. "What could be more Christian than helping the economically disadvantaged and underserved? Jesus was all about lifting up the poor and oppressed, right? So He would have been all in favour of giving the world's struggling nations access to technology that would help put them on an equal footing with former colonizers. John Sotero grew up in Brazil, which is considered an 'emerging' or 'developing' nation. Although things are improving, there is a lot of work still to be done before countries such as Brazil can compete on an even keel with the rest of the world. So no, our position is that Senator Charles' objections were not religious, but rather of a purely utilitarian and economic nature –"

"And then some kooky performance artist troupe in Montreal," Baher interrupted, "where you – and by you, I mean where LuNation Mining

International are based, decided to go ahead and call him out on his hypocrisy."

"Right," Mia replied. "Montreal has long been a haven for offbeat comedy and subversive art."

"Yes," Baher agreed. "I remember where there used to be an annual comedy festival every summer. I've even given a few shows there when it was still a thing. But this point you're making, that Senator Charles' objections are not religious, makes for a good segue to introduce my next guest, Betty Vaughan, who is Senator Charles' Chief of Staff and spokesperson."

Ah, so Vaughan got a promotion.

"Welcome, Betty," Baher said, to feeble applause from the audience.

"Thank you Will," Vaughan replied in her Southern drawl. "Glad to be here."

Mia looked up at the giant screen on the wall opposite the desk and saw the familiar image of a meticulously coiffed twenty-something blonde with dark roots, her wan complexion aglow with excessive quantities of bronzer, her lithe and toned frame draped in a tight-fitting, sleeveless power suit dress. Her gratuitously ample cleavage framed a large gold cross hanging prominently from around her neck.

"And thank you for agreeing to take part in our show this evening," Baher continued. "I know that our audience is not necessarily one that agrees with Senator Charles and his recent position, so thank you for your grit."

"It's my pleasure, Will," Vaughan said demurely. "And before we start, I'd like to thank Mia for agreeing to speak to me this evening, and for being so brave in the face of all that's happened in the last seven days."

Ah, so PR Barbie is also well trained in the craft of moonshine, Mia thought, resisting the urge to theatrically snort a sip of water from the mug the production assistant placed before her. *Let the games begin.*

"And from my understanding," Baher said, "you and Mia have never spoken directly to each other before until tonight?"

"That's right," Vaughan answered.

158

"All right," Baher continued. "Then let's get to it. Before we even get to the other video that went viral this week, the one about the protesters staging a Witches' Sabbat in the woods north of Montreal to rally behind Mia after some of Senator Charles' supporters threatened her life... what is your response to what Mia just said? That your boss, Senator Charles, objects to LuNation's mission statement because of economic reasons and not religious ones?"

"Well, Will," Vaughan replied, "first off, let me just say to Mia that we are all very sorry that some folks went too far and threatened your life, even though –"

"Even though Senator Charles never once condemned the people who were chanting for my death since last Friday's press conference?" Mia interrupted.

"Senator Ethan Charles is a godly man, and he would never condone any form of violence against anyone, even someone like yourself, Ms. Thorne," Vaughan replied.

"Someone like myself?" Mia asked. "Do you mean a former journalist? A member of the free press? Or do you mean someone who worked at an alternative spirituality magazine? Come now, let's be honest. The good Senator jumped on the whole religion bandwagon to distract from his true motives for opposing my employer's work. So why don't you answer's Will question? How *do* you respond to allegations that Senator Charles started this whole mess months ago because he stands to lose a lot of money if LuNation succeeds in bringing free, clean energy to large parts of the globe?"

"This is misdirection, and you know it," Vaughan replied, barely concealing her annoyance. "As I said, Senator Charles is a godly man, and he opposes anything that goes against God's plan. And I know that John Sotero knows this, and I wouldn't be surprised if LuNation Mining International were responsible for staging and releasing both videos – the one with the fake Christian crazy lady at the steakhouse and the goofy Satanic ritual in the woods!"

"LuNation Mining International categorically denies any involvement with the production of either video you mentioned," Mia retorted, "and despite the repeated cease-and-desist letters Mr. Sotero sent to your boss' office over the last few months, Senator Charles persists in slandering LuNation's CEO and founder, a well-known philanthropist and visionary. And it bears repeating that the allegations posted on Senator Charles' website in early May are completely unfounded, and we suspect that their only purpose was to serve the Senator's agenda to tank LuNation Mining International's stock and to undermine our credibility on the world stage. Let me be abundantly clear, *Elizabeth*, Senator Charles' campaign of lies against Mr. Sotero and LuNation Mining Internations constitutes libel under Canadian law, and if the Senator persist in his 'witch-hunt'," Mia said, using air quotes for emphasis, "we will have to pursue legal action."

"Anything Senator Charles has ever said about John Sotero and LuNation Mining International," Vaughan replied, "is free speech, and therefore protected."

"Under Canadian law, *hate* speech, which can cause real harm and incite others to violence, is not protected," Mia said.

"And what about what *you* said about Senator Charles last week, Mia?" Vaughan inquired. "Some might say that *your* press conference from LuNation's headquarters absolutely constitutes slander against Senator Charles, wouldn't you say?"

"It's not slander if everything I said can be proven true," Mia replied.

"It is my understanding," Baher interjected, "that John Sotero repeatedly invited Senator Charles to meet with him at his corporate headquarters in Southern Quebec to resolve this feud in person, man-to-man, isn't that true, Mia?"

"That's right, Will," Mia agreed. "However, Senator Charles has repeatedly and categorically declined to travel to Canada, for some odd reason –"

"That's because of that last, ridiculous video," Vaughan retorted. "The one with the Satanists in the woods riling up the Canadian social justice warriors against Ethan, who would have him –"

"Burned at the stake?" Mia quipped. "Just as Senator Charles' supporters would have done to me, *with his blessing*?"

"Senator Charles is a godly man –"

"Who was caught on camera grinning ear to ear when his supporters began chanting 'Burn the Witch!'" Baher said. "Even a good Christian such as yourself ought to agree that this is unbecoming of a godly man, as you insist Senator Charles to be."

"Precisely," Mia agreed.

"And the thing about video," Baher continued, "especially in this day and age, is that once it's out there, you can never coax the genie back into the bottle."

"I assure you!" Vaughan shrieked, "Senator Charles is a man of God –"

"Are you certain of that?" Will asked. "Because if there's one thing I hate, it's people who hide behind their God and the Bible to commit and condone the most repugnant acts, while they themselves are far from pure and godly. And it has recently come to our attention that there is another video proving Mia's allegations that Senator Ethan Charles is anything but the good, pious Christian he would have his constituents believe him to be. A warning to our viewers, this next video is quite graphic, but this is GAN so you all know what you've bought into when you subscribed to this network. Tina, roll the tape."

On the screen opposite Baher's interview desk, the flushed, giant face of Betty Vaughan gave way to a somewhat grainy video footage of a gathering where the attendees wore the colourful and elaborate vestments of the group Mia privately referred to as the House of Interstellar Intercourse.

"So, just to be clear," Baher narrated over the footage, "what we're looking at is a recording of a fertility ritual? A fertility ritual of some sort of a well-known alternative spirituality group, to use Mia's expression, with chapters in Quebec and in Europe, celebrating the Feast of Eros. This, I am told, is a ceremony involving a rite of sympathetic magic to bring love and peace to all living beings on this planet and every other planet. So yeah, it's a sexy space cult. Their name is not important, but their relevance to this conversation will become clear just about... now. Here, on the left, you see a younger Ethan Charles, a few years before he got involved in U.S. politics, participating in this ceremony, which I am also told is not open to outsiders except by invitation, or through large donations to their Foundation to fund research into human cloning. Ah, there we are."

Baher paused, letting the audience gasp at varying volumes.

"That's a whole lot of penis!" some wag blurted out, to which the audience responded with peels of laughter.

"And what was Ethan Charles doing in Quebec at the time, you may ask?" Baher continued. "Police reports obtained by our affiliates in Montreal through the Access to Information Act, dated one day after the video was taken, confirm that Senator Charles was on his way back from touring his oil drilling installations in the Canadian Western provinces. Then for some reason he made a pit stop halfway across the second largest country in the world to threaten his ex-wife, who now resides in Quebec and has become a naturalized Canadian citizen. And this video was taken on the night of his arrest, when the RCMP apprehended him outside the... temple? Okay, let's call it a temple. They arrested him after the space orgy climaxed and he got put on a permanent no-fly list ever since. This might be why he refused to meet John Sotero in Canada face-to-face and settle the matter like adults, because he's permanently banned from entering the country."

"Wow," Mia said once the video footage went dark on the screen and was replaced by a very pale-looking Betty Vaughan. "That was... a lot."

"So there you have it, folks," Baher said. "Senator Ethan Charles may be a lot of things, but a stalwart paragon of Christian values, he is not.

"And it was Willow Raven," Mia interjected before Baher could continue, "the editor-in chief of *Goddess Digest Magazine*, who planned the recent ritual in the woods north of Montreal, not John Sotero."

"Right," Baher agreed. "And whatever Willow Raven intended by staging her ritual that went nuclear on social media this week, it must have worked because this video was sent to us anonymously the day after the so-called "goofy" ritual in the woods was broadcast live on the news. And let me be clear – Willow Raven is in no way, shape, or form affiliated with LuNation Mining International, isn't that right, Mia?"

"That's correct," Mia replied, "except for the fact that I briefly worked for her as a junior journalist when I was fresh out of graduate school. Willow is a wondrously kind woman, who cares deeply about her staff and dotes on them like her own children, even after we've left her employ."

"Now, to address the magical unicorn in the room," Baher commented. "Taking a job at *Goddess Digest Magazine* was not exactly your first choice when you finished your graduate studies, was it not?"

"No, Will, it was not... not exactly," Mia answered diplomatically.

"I get it," Baher replied. "All of us have had to take jobs from time to time that we ended up regretting – I know I have, but that's just how life is sometimes. At least that is true for those of us who work for a living, and don't have rich parents with lots of connections to land their kids cushy jobs right out of College. But I digress. The release of this latest video in the saga of Senator Charles begs the question: *what else* has the good Senator been keeping from his constituents? What other shenanigans has he been hiding behind his completely manufactured pious image? What other skeletons, whether or not of this Earth, will we find in his closet? Betty? What do you have to say about what you and the audience here and at home just saw?"

"I... ah..." Vaughan stammered, having completely lost her nerve.

"And that's all the time we have for tonight," Baher said. "I would like to thank my guests, Mia Thorne, and Betty Vaughan; next week I'll be interviewing His Holiness Pope Horkos of the Discordians, and if you're watching this online, don't forget to click 'like' and subscribe. Good night and see you next week!"

Mia heaved a sigh of relief as the hip-hop theme music blasted loudly from the speakers in the soundstage to the audience's standing ovation.

Shaking Baher's hand as she got up to exit the stage, Mia mouthed the words "Thank you".

"Hey," Baher replied, following her backstage. "It was the least I could do after the producers sprang Betty Vaughan on us at the last minute. I wasn't too happy about it either, but I thought this might be well worth it in the end. No hard feelings?"

"No hard feelings," Mia said with utmost gratitude.

"Just remember me when your boss starts taking names of reporters and dignitaries to bring along on his next flight to the Moon!"

"Will do," Mia said at last, secure in the knowledge that Baher had no idea that it was, in fact, Alex who leaked the space orgy sex tape to the GAN executives after a prudent five-day waiting period following Hathor's visit to the LuNation Mining International headquarters at the beginning of the week.

The golden apple is cast.

Marisol Charbonneau

Chapter Twenty-Three

On the eve of Lughnassadh, the halfway point between the summer solstice and the autumn equinox, Mia tidied up her garden, having already rendered her new home presentable for the imminent arrival of her friends and colleagues. As the ancients Celts marked the harvest of the first fruits of the season on this day, Mia thought the date auspicious for hosting her housewarming party as well as a celebration of another milestone marking LuNation's victory over their unworthy foe. In the months following that fateful press conference set into motion by Operation Moonshine last May, U.S. and Canadian law enforcement agencies began investigating Senator Ethan Charles for obstruction of justice for his oil empire's involvement in covering up the abduction and sexual assault of many Indigenous women in the North American oilpatch. Federal police in both countries also uncovered a bevy of additional cover-ups with regards to non-compliance of environmental regulations and other egregious displays of corruption. For these reasons, and all the personal and corporate lawsuits that ensued, Charles resigned from his position in the U.S. Senate and withdrew from public life in disgrace, pending trial.

Within hours of her impassioned speech at LuNation's press conference, broadcast across the world by all forms of media, Mia became an instant Internet sensation. For months, her likeness launched a thousand memes, and feminists and social justice warriors of all stripes claimed her public persona as an avatar of righteous female fury at the deplorable avidity of powerful men who would hold back the rest of the world to satisfy their insatiable greed. Despite her sudden fame borne of an elaborate yet necessary deception, Mia remained humble in her newfound purpose, grateful for her stable employment at a company whose ideals aligned very much with her own.

Her employment was also quite lucrative, allowing her to purchase a modest house, a cottage really, in Mont-Saint-Hilaire, in the shadows of the Sacred Mountain, a short distance from LuNation Mining International's South Shore campus. Having spent the bulk of her advance to pay off the remainder of her student loans, Mia purchased this fixer-upper for a song, ignoring rumours that the hedge at the back of the yard was haunted.

There would be plenty of time in weeks to come for renovations and exorcisms. But now, as Mia's guests would soon begin to trickle in, the time had come to finally libate at the large tree at the edge of the driveway, behind the shed and hidden from view of the neighbours. After all these months, Mia could scarce remember all the gods and goddesses she hoped to honour with her libation, so instead she muttered a prayer of thanks to all the spirits of earth, sea, and sky as she poured the remainder of the liquor she purchased months ago, on the way back to Willowdale from an improbable midday traffic jam on the 15 North on a grey Wednesday afternoon. Mia smiled as the precious liquid fell upon the tree's upraised roots, realizing that her lips had barely touched the brew since her employment at LuNation began. She also managed somehow to shed her remaining extra pounds since then, as if her flesh at last relinquished the burden of her self-doubt.

Once the task was done, Mia placed the empty bottles in the recycling bin, and went back inside her house to remove trays of snacks and crudités from her kitchen and place them on the dining room table. She was disappointed that Hester and her extended family could not be there with her for this celebration, as this year Lughnassadh coincided with Tish'a B'Av. However, Mia knew they would all be there in spirit. Besides, it would have been crass to insist upon their attendance, considering that the holiday required a 25-hour religious fast.

John and Maggie were the first to arrive, carpooling with Alex from opulent Westmount in the hills of Montreal. They brought with them elaborately crafted salads and finger foods from a professional catering service, which made Mia's packaged snacks look downright indigent in comparison. For once, Mia didn't mind the wealth discrepancy between herself and Alex, or even the Soteros, as she felt uncharacteristically grateful for the things she did have, and for the friends she made along the way. Allen and Erinna came by soon after, followed by Othmane and Mary Jane who brought Phil and Katie with them. Phil told Mia that Willow sent her regards and her congratulations for her good work, yet regretfully could not be present due to work engagements.

Of course.

Dr. Seth Hollander arrived shortly thereafter with a caravan of LuNation co-workers, causing Mia to wonder whether her little house might burst from all the people crowding every nook and cranny. She then kindly asked some of her guests to follow her to the sparsely furnished backyard patio, bidding them to bring the copious amounts of food they all brought to the party. Apparently, no one seemed to mind that Mia's home looked like a cabin where one could imagine a woods witch would live.

Well, they would not be wrong...

In the last few months, Mia often wondered whether she did, in fact, bend the Universe to her will on the day she became stranded with Allen and Erinna on the 15 North on route to a needlessly tedious assignment with the Oracle. Now that Mia thought about it, it almost seemed as though the Oracle herself had foreseen this outcome, and told Willow about it, albeit in a weirdly cryptic manner. Perhaps this was why Willow had been so overbearing with Mia on the day she left her position at Willowdale, and why she continued to avoid her to this day. As far as Mia was concerned, if Phil and Katie still spoke to her and visited, Willow could avoid her until the end of time. Mia had long since made arrangements to dispose of her moribund car stored somewhere in the West of Montreal, and shortly thereafter instructed Erinna to donate whatever belongings of hers remained at Willowdale to a women's shelter, as she had no use for reminders of a less pleasant time in her life.

Perhaps some things are better left unknown.

"Hey Mia," Alex said from inside the kitchen. "Want me to pour you a cup of sangria?"

Mia turned around and saw Alex, Erinna and Mary Jane pouring chopped fruit and several bottles of juices and wine into a large mixing bowl.

Interesting. I now have my very own coven of witches in my kitchen, ready to do my bidding.

"Sure," Mia replied. "Double, double toil and trouble..." she muttered as she stepped inside the kitchen through the patio door.

Mary Jane smiled. "Fire burn, and cauldron bubble!" she added with a laugh.

"You know your Bible *and* your Shakespeare?" Erinna commented. "What else are you holding out on us?"

"If I told you," Mary Jane replied, "I'd have to kill you."

"I can't be listening to this," Alex said. "Not if you ever decide to hire me as your counsel."

"Okay, enough murder talk," Mia said. "I was told there would be sangria!"

"Here you go," Alex said, handing Mia a full cup.

Mia took a sip. "The nectar of the gods!" she proclaimed loudly.

"I hope you don't mind," Mary Jane said. "We looked through your cabinets for your liquor. We wanted to make margaritas but couldn't find anything."

"You're not turning into a teetotaler, are you Mia?" Erinna asked.

"Say that three times fast!" Alex joked.

"Not really," Mia answered. "I'm just cutting back. I'm not going full abstinence here." She took another sip of her sangria.

"We made enough for an army because I thought you might want to libate whatever's left," Alex said.

"There won't be any left!" Seth joked from the small counter separating the kitchen from the living room. "Are you ladies coming or what? They're about to show footage of the *Selene* team breaking ground!"

"Oh, shit, yeah!" Mia stammered. "Almost forgot about that!"

"Isn't that why you brought us all together?" Seth asked.

"There is also the matter of my housewarming party," Mia protested. "John could have thrown a ground-breaking party at headquarters but decided not to, given that it's a Saturday and all."

"And we pretty much owe this all to Mia," Alex interjected. "Now make yourself useful and help me put this sangria on that counter. I'll get the cups, MJ please get the ladle and the paper towels. This might get messy."

Seth complied, while Mia reminded the guests on her patio about the other housewarming party on the Moon.

"You know," Maggie told Seth as she poured herself a cup of sangria. "They're not so much breaking ground as setting up base camp in a lunar cave. But it's an important first step!"

"Hear, hear!" John agreed from his spot in the middle of the couch.

No one else dared to sit next to him, leaving the two available cushions for Maggie and, presumably, Mia. As soon as Mia entered the living room, the guests grew quiet, taking their seats on the floor or on the chairs around the dining room table. John turned around and gestured for Mia to take her seat beside him. When Mia offered her seat to another guest, Allen and Alex flanked her to escort her to the couch.

"Okay, fine!" Mia said finally as she sat next to John. "But I get to wield the remote!"

Katie, who sat right in front of the coffee table, grabbed the device and promptly handed it to Mia.

"M'lady," the child said facetiously.

Mia smiled. "At ease," she replied, cranking up the volume on the television for everyone to hear.

After a few minutes of unnecessary commentary from the talking heads inside the idiot box, a retired astronaut currently consulting for the Canadian Space Agency remarked on the many ways in which LuNation Mining International's activities would benefit all of humanity.

"You talked about that in your speech three months ago, didn't you?" Katie asked Mia.

"Yeah," Mia answered. "That was the goal of the United Nations Outer Space Treaty since the beginning of the Space Race!"

"You know," Alex said, half-seated on the couch's armrest next to Mia. "It's not too late for you to start studying Space Law!"

"Study Space Law?" Mia replied. "I told you I only memorized the Moon Treaty and the Outer Space Treaty because they read like Homeric hymns! I don't have the mind for legalese, not by a long shot. Besides, I wouldn't want to end up having *you* as my boss! That would be weird."

"I think we're way beyond weird," Allen said, to everyone's agreement.

"Guys!" Katie called out. "Look!"

All heads turned once more to the television screen, where the news studio yielded to a crystal-clear satellite image of a comely woman putting on her helmet while two of her colleagues awaited, already fully clad in astronaut gear. Once the woman's helmet was satisfactorily put in place, someone behind her opened the airlock, and the group stepped outside on the lunar surface.

"We are standing on a particularly oxygen-rich deposit of regolith," a woman said while her colleagues bounced ahead in front of her in slow motion. "This will help power our first wave of equipment, until we've deployed enough solar panels to take over the task. Now Gillian over there is standing on the spot where we will start laying our solar panel farm, all the way to the lunar horizon. Wave hi, Gill?"

The bouncy astronaut who appeared the farthest from the camera turned around and waved.

"I think this is far enough. Barry?" said the same woman, whose name Mia had not caught during the broadcast.

The camera spanned 180 degrees, revealing a low rise on the lunar surface beneath an ink-black sky. At the bottom of the rise there appeared a pair of white double doors that seemed to blend almost perfectly with the monochromatic moonscape, except for the small yet starkly visible LuNation Mining International corporate logo.

"So this is home sweet home," Barry, the man holding the camera, said. "For at least the next couple of years while we lay the groundwork for our secondary habitat after we run out of Moon caves in the region. It will have to be built like a bunker to withstand radiation and meteor impacts. And there's all that Moon dust –"

"The cave looks like a Rebel base," Katie commented, eliciting laughter from everyone gathered in Mia's living room.

"In a way it is, dear," Maggie said. "And we will have the home advantage when the time comes to defeat the evil Empire once it strikes back!"

"Hail Victory!" Erinna bellowed.

"Hail!" a half-dozen guest replied in unison, greatly confusing the others.

"And hail Mia, whose spin-doctoring not only helped our company's shares recover on the stock market, but also skyrocket over the summer!" John said.

This time, the whole room erupted into a collective "HAIL MIA!"

Mia blushed, her eyes fixed on the image of the silvery Moon on her television screen.

"You're welcome," she whispered, without a hint of hubris.

Marisol Charbonneau

www.ingramcontent.com/pod-product-compliance
Lightning Source LLC
Chambersburg PA
CBHW051822170626

46807CB00003B/981